His eyes came back to hers, his inherent cynicism glittering like black diamonds.

'I can only assume my father thought by forcing me to marry his little nursemaid it might have some sort of reforming effect on me,' he said. 'What do you think, Miss March? Do your skills extend to taming decadent playboys?'

Melanie Milburne says: 'I am married to a surgeon, Steve, and have two gorgeous sons, Paul and Phil. I live in Hobart, Tasmania, where I enjoy an active life as a long-distance runner and a nationally ranked top ten Master's swimmer. I also have a Master's Degree in Education, but my children totally turned me off the idea of teaching! When not running or swimming I write, and when I'm not doing all of the above I'm reading. And if someone could invent a way for me to read during a four-kilometre swim I'd be even happier!'

Recent titles by the same author:

THE MARCIANO LOVE-CHILD
INNOCENT WIFE, BABY OF SHAME
ANDROLETTI'S MISTRESS
WILLINGLY BEDDED, FORCIBLY WEDDED
BOUGHT FOR HER BABY
BEDDED AND WEDDED FOR REVENGE
THE VIRGIN'S PRICE

The Royal House of Niroli:

SURGEON PRINCE, ORDINARY WIFE *(Book 2)*

Did you know that Melanie also writes for Medical™ Romance?

SINGLE DAD SEEKS A WIFE
  (The Brides of Penhally Bay)
THE SURGEON BOSS'S BRIDE
HER MAN OF HONOUR
IN HER BOSS'S SPECIAL CARE
A DOCTOR BEYOND COMPARE

THE FIORENZA
FORCED MARRIAGE

BY
MELANIE MILBURNE

MILLS & BOON®
Pure reading pleasure™

All the characters in this book have no existence outside the imagination of the author, and have no relation whatsoever to anyone bearing the same name or names. They are not even distantly inspired by any individual known or unknown to the author, and all the incidents are pure invention.

First published in Great Britain 2008
Harlequin Mills & Boon Limited,
Eton House, 18-24 Paradise Road, Richmond, Surrey TW9 1SR

© Melanie Milburne 2008

ISBN: 978 0 263 86484 7

Set in Times Roman 10½ on 12¼ pt
01-1208-54596

Printed and bound in Spain
by Litografia Rosés, S.A., Barcelona

THE FIORENZA
FORCED MARRIAGE

To one of my most loyal fans, Anu Sankaran, who has encouraged me from book one. Thank you so much for your lovely e-mails and fabulous personal reviews! This one is just for you. x

CHAPTER ONE

EMMA looked at the Italian lawyer in heart-stopping shock. 'There must be some sort of m-mistake,' she said, her voice wobbling with disbelief. 'How could I possibly be included in Signore Fiorenza's will? I was just his carer.'

'It is no mistake,' Francesca Rossi said, pointedly tapping the thick document in front of her. 'I have it here in black and white. Valentino Fiorenza changed his will a matter of weeks before he died.'

Emma sat in a stunned silence. She had lived with and nursed the multimillionaire for eighteen months and not once had she thought something like this would happen. 'But I don't understand…' she said after a moment. 'Why on earth would he leave me half of his estate?'

'That's exactly what his son has been asking,' Francesca Rossi said with a speaking glance. 'I believe he is on his way over from London as we speak. As his father's only remaining heir one can only assume he was expecting The Villa Fiorenza and the bulk of his father's assets to pass directly to him.'

Emma chewed at her bottom lip for a moment. 'You said the terms of the will are rather strange….'

'They are quite unusual,' Francesca agreed. 'In order to

inherit your share you must be legally married to Rafaele Fiorenza within a month and stay married to him for a year.'

Emma felt her stomach drop like a gymnast mistiming a tricky manoeuvre on the bar. 'M-married in a month?' she croaked. *'For a year?'*

'Yes, otherwise the estate in its entirety will automatically pass to a previous mistress of Valentino's, a woman by the name of Sondra Henning. Did he ever mention her to you?'

Emma wrinkled her brow. 'No, I don't think so…but then he was a very private man. He didn't talk much about anything, especially towards the end.'

The lawyer leafed through the document before looking back up at Emma. 'Signore Fiorenza stipulated that upon marriage to his son you are to receive a lump sum of fifty thousand euros, and then for every year you remain married to Rafaele you will receive an allowance,' she said. 'A rather generous one, in fact.'

Emma's stomach did another fall from the bar. 'H-how generous?'

The lawyer named a sum that sent Emma's brows shooting upwards. 'I guess it does seem rather a lot to walk away from…' she said, thinking of her sister's recent phone call. Fifty thousand euros at the current exchange rate would not completely solve Simone's financial situation, but it would certainly go a long way to help her get back on her feet.

'It is a lot to walk away from,' Francesca said. 'Even without factoring in the allowance, the villa, as you know from staying there, is considered one of the most beautiful show-pieces around Lake Como. You would be a fool to forfeit such an asset, even a half share of it.'

'What is Rafaele Fiorenza like…I mean as a person?' Emma asked. 'I've seen photos of him in the press from time to time, but his father barely mentioned him. And as far as I know he wasn't at the funeral. I got the feeling there was bad blood between them.'

'I have not met him personally,' Francesca said. 'Apparently he left home when he was a young adult to study abroad. He is a high-flying stock trader now. But, yes, as you said he is often featured in gossip magazines throughout Europe and further abroad. Word has it he is a bit of a playboy and a very wealthy one at that.'

'Yes, I did get that impression,' Emma said, and then with another little crease of her brow added, 'but what if he doesn't agree to the terms of his father's will? If he's so wealthy why would he agree to be married to a perfect stranger?'

'The entire estate involves a great deal of money, even for a rich man,' Francesca said. 'Besides, the villa was where he spent most of his early childhood until he went to boarding school abroad. I cannot see him walking away from such a gold mine without at least inspecting the candidate his father chose to be his bride.'

Emma felt every fine hair on her body lift up like the fur of a startled cat. 'I haven't said I would agree to marry anyone,' she said, 'especially a man who didn't even have the decency to visit or communicate with his dying father.'

'Given he has had little or no contact with his father for the last decade or so you might have a hard time explaining your relationship,' Francesca said. 'I know you were employed as Valentino's carer but the press haven't always seen it that way and neither, I suspect, will Rafaele Fiorenza.'

Emma straightened agitatedly in her chair. When she had first taken on the position as Valentino Fiorenza's carer she had not been prepared for how the press would misinterpret her relationship with him. Every time she had accompanied him out in public it seemed the paparazzi were there to document it, often times misconstruing the situation to make her appear a gold-digger, content to hook up with a man three times her age. She still cringed as she thought of the last photo that had appeared in the press. Weakened by the progression of his bone cancer Valentino had been too proud to use a walking stick and had relied increasingly on Emma's support. The photographer had captured a moment where Emma's arms had gone around her employer's waist to keep him from falling, making it appear she was intimately involved with him. Even her sister Simone had rung her from Australia and asked if what everyone was saying was true.

'He can think what he likes, but there was absolutely nothing improper about my relationship with his father,' Emma said. 'Valentino was an invalid, for pity's sake. He employed me to take care of his day-to-day needs. I grew fond of him certainly, but that happens with just about every home care client I take on. Looking after someone as they count down their last days is incredibly poignant. I know it's not wise to become emotionally involved, but from the very first day Valentino Fiorenza struck me as a very lonely soul. He had wealth but not health and happiness.'

'Well, let us hope Rafaele Fiorenza understands the situation,' Francesca said. 'In the meantime I take it you are staying on at the villa?'

'Yes,' Emma said. 'I wasn't sure what else to do. Some of the staff have taken leave and I didn't want the place left unattended until I heard from the son. I've been looking for alternative accommodation but with not much luck so far. I let my previous lease go as Signore Fiorenza insisted I move in with him from day one.'

'You do realise of course that Rafaele Fiorenza stands to lose rather a lot if you do not agree to the terms,' Francesca said in a serious tone. 'Even though he might not need the money it would still be wise to take some time to think it over before you come to a final decision for his sake as well as your own.'

Emma shifted uncomfortably in her chair. 'I realise it is a difficult situation for him…but I'm not sure I can agree to such a thing. It doesn't seem…right…'

'There are a lot of people who would see it differently,' the lawyer said. 'They would not baulk at a short term marriage of convenience in exchange for a fortune.'

Emma nibbled at her bottom lip for a moment. 'You mentioned the marriage has to last a year. Is there any way of negotiating on that time frame?'

'No, I am afraid not, but, as I said earlier, for every year you remain married to Rafaele you will be paid an allowance.' Francesca rolled back her office chair and offered her hand across the desk. 'I hope it goes well for you whatever you decide, Miss March,' she said. 'Signore Fiorenza Senior was clearly very fond of you. He would not have been an easy person to nurse, I would imagine. The Fiorenza family has had its share of tragedy. The boys' mother died when they were very young children and if that was not bad enough the younger of the two boys, Giovanni, died in a tragic accident when he was about eight. Over the years Signore Fiorenza became increasingly bitter and reclusive, not to mention terribly stubborn.'

'Yes, he was certainly stubborn,' Emma said. 'But I couldn't help feeling it was all a bit of a front. He liked to rant and rave a lot but he was as soft as butter towards the end. I really liked him. I will miss him.'

'You never know, Miss March, the son may turn out to be perfect husband material,' the lawyer said with a wry smile. 'It would not be the first time a marriage of convenience in this country turned into something else entirely.'

Emma backed out of the lawyer's office with a strained

smile and made her way to the bank of lifts. But all the way down to the ground floor she felt a fluttery sensation disturbing the lining of her stomach, like a thousand tiny moths all frantically looking for a way out…

Every time Emma stepped through the elaborate wrought-iron gates of the Villa Fiorenza she stood for a moment or two in awe. The massive gardens set on four tiers were nothing short of breathtaking, the lush green of yew hedges and elm and beech trees and cypress pines a perfect backdrop for the crimson and pinks and reds of azaleas and roses and other fragrant spring blooms. The villa itself was equally breathtaking; set above the stunning crystal-blue beauty of Lake Como, it was four storeys high and built in the neo-classical style lending it an allure of old-world grandeur that never failed to take Emma's breath away.

Most of the rooms of the villa were no longer in use, the antique furniture draped in shroud-like sheets and the shutters pulled tight across the sightless windows, giving the grand old place a slightly haunted look. And without the presence of daily staff bustling about the villa and gardens the sense of loneliness and isolation was even more acute.

After she had spent more than a year looking after him in his palazzo in Milan, Valentino Fiorenza had announced to Emma six weeks ago he wanted to come back to the villa to die. And now to Emma it seemed as if every breath of breeze that disturbed the leaves on the trees were lamenting his passing. She had loved spending time pushing him around the gardens in his wheelchair, for, although towards the end he had found speech difficult, she had sensed his enjoyment of the peaceful surroundings.

The warmth of the spring weather brought out the heady scent of wisteria and jasmine as Emma walked under the arbour on the second tier of the gardens. She had just stopped to dead-head some of the milk-white climbing roses when a sleek black sports car growled throatily as it turned into the driveway at the back of the villa, like a panther returning to its lair.

She brushed a loose strand of hair out of her eyes and watched as a tall figure unfolded himself from the car. Even from this distance she could see the likeness to his father immediately: the loose-limbed, rangy build, the brooding frown, the chiselled jaw and the arrogant set to his mouth all spoke of a man used to insisting on and getting his own way. But, unlike his father, Rafaele Fiorenza was well over six feet tall and his fit body wasn't bent over double and ravaged by disease and his glossy black curly hair was thick and plenti-ful on his head and held no trace of grey. It was casually styled, the wide, deep grooves in amongst the strands suggest-ing he had used his fingers as its most recent combing tool.

Even though Emma had seen his photograph in the press a couple of times she realised now it hadn't done him justice. He was quite simply the most arrestingly handsome man she had ever seen.

He was dressed in casual trousers and an open-necked light blue shirt, the cuffs rolled back over his strong tanned forearms, an expensive-looking silver watch around his left wrist and a pair of designer sunglasses, which shielded the ex-pression in his eyes.

He slammed the car door and strode down the steps leading to the second tier, his long, purposeful strides bringing him within a matter of seconds to where she was unconsciously crumbling rose petals in her hand. 'Miss March, I presume?' he said in a clipped, distinctly unfriendly tone.

Emma hated talking to people wearing sunglasses, particu-larly the one-way lens type he was wearing. She always felt at a disadvantage not being able to read what was going on behind that impenetrable screen. She lifted her chin and let the petals float to the ground at her feet. 'Yes, that is correct,' she said. 'I take it you are Rafaele Fiorenza.'

He removed the sunglasses, his black-brown gaze sweeping over her contemptuously. 'And I take it you were my father's latest floozy.'

Emma automatically stiffened. 'I take it you have been misinformed, Signore Fiorenza,' she returned with arctic chill. 'I was employed as your father's carer.'

He gave her a cynical smile but it didn't involve his dark bottomless brown eyes. 'So you took care of all of his physical needs, did you, Miss March?' he said. 'I must confess my mind is having a bit of a field day with that information.'

'Then I would say your mind needs to drag itself out of the gutter, Signore Fiorenza,' she returned with a deliberately haughty look.

His smile went from cynical to devilish. 'So how do you feel about becoming my bride, Miss March?'

Emma tightened her mouth. 'I have no intention of doing any such thing.'

He stood looking down at her for a pulsing silence, his eyes unwavering as they held hers. Emma tried her best not to squirm under his piercing scrutiny but in the end she was the first to drop her gaze.

'I suppose you put him up to it, did you?' he asked. 'In a weak moment of his you talked him into signing away a fortune.'

'That's a despicable thing to say,' she said, looking back at him in affront. 'I had no idea what he had planned. The first I heard of it was when his legal firm contacted me about the terms of the will.'

'Do not take me for a fool,' he said. 'You were living with my father for a year and a half. That is the longest relationship he has had since my mother died. Everyone knows you were sleeping with him. It has been in the papers numerous times.'

Emma felt her cheeks burning but forced herself to hold his gaze. 'I did not have that sort of relationship with your father. The press made it up just to sell extra copies. They do that with anyone rich or famous.'

His dark eyes glittered with disdain. 'Come on, now, Miss March,' he said. 'You surely do not expect me to believe my father wrote you into his will at the last moment just because you smiled sweetly at him on his deathbed, do you?'

Emma sent him a flinty glare. 'I have never slept with your father. It's totally preposterous of you to even suggest it.'

His expression communicated his disbelief. 'My father was a well-known womaniser,' he said. 'You lived with him for well over a year before he publicly announced he was ill. It would be all too easy to assume you wormed your way into his bed to secure yourself a fortune.'

'I did no such thing!' she protested hotly. 'I only agreed to live with your father so long before his health deteriorated because he didn't want a profusion of carers coming in and out of his life. He was also concerned if people knew he was terminally ill when he was first diagnosed, his investment clients would leave him in droves. His illness progressed slowly at first, but a couple of months ago he realised the end was near. I did my best to support him through the final stages.'

'I just bet you did,' he said with a little curl of his lip. 'Although I must say you are not his usual type. He usually went for busty, brassy blondes. Pint-sized brunettes must have been a taste he had recently acquired.'

Emma felt the scorch of his dark gaze run over her again and inwardly seethed. 'I resent your reprehensible insinuations,' she said. 'I can see now why your father refused to even have your name mentioned in his presence. You have absolutely appalling manners.'

He had the audacity to laugh at her. 'What a prim little schoolmarm you are,' he taunted. 'Miss March suits you perfectly. I bet my father loved you putting him to bed.'

Emma was almost beyond speech and to her immense irritation she could feel her face flaming. 'You…you have no right to speak to me like—'

'I have every right, Miss March.' He cut her off rudely. 'My father would not marry you, would he? He swore he would never marry again after my mother died. But you obviously thought of a way to get your hands on the Fiorenza fortune by suggesting you marry me instead.'

Emma clenched her teeth as she battled to contain her temper. 'You are the very last man I would consent to marry,' she threw at him heatedly.

His eyes were like twin lasers as they held hers. 'You want more money, is that it, Miss March? I am sure I can afford you. Just tell me how much you want and I will write you a cheque here and now.'

Emma bristled at his effrontery. 'You think you can wave your wallet around and pay me?'

He gave her a scornful smile. 'That is the language of women such as you. You saw a big fat cherry just ripe for the picking in my father, did you not? You must have buttered him up rather well to get him to rewrite his will. I wonder what tricks you had up your sleeve, or should I say skirt?'

Emma had never felt closer to slapping a person. She curled her hands into fists, fighting for control, anger bubbling up inside her at his despicable taunts. 'How dare you?' she bit out.

He rocked back on his heels in an imperious manner. 'You are quite the little firebrand behind that demure façade, eh, Miss March? No wonder my father took such a shine to you.

Who knows? We might make quite a match of it after all. I like my women hot and flustered. I think you might do very well as my bride.'

Emma gave him a look that could strip paint. 'You are the most obnoxious man I have ever met,' she bit out. 'Do you really think I would agree to become involved with someone like you?'

He gave her another cynical smile. 'I am not sure I should tell you what I think right now, Miss March,' he drawled. 'You might follow through on your current desire to slap my face.'

Emma hated that she had been so transparent. It made her feel he had an advantage over her being able to read her body language so well. What else could he see? she wondered. Could he tell she was deeply disturbed by his arrant masculinity? That his sensually shaped mouth made her lips tingle at the thought of what it would feel like to have him kiss her?

Her reaction to him was somewhat of a bewildering shock to her. She was normally such a sensible, level-headed person. She had never considered herself a sensualist, but then she had so little experience when it came to men.

Rafaele Fiorenza, on the other hand, looked as if he had loads of experience when it came to women. His tall frame, classically handsome features and magnetic dark brown eyes with their impossibly long dark lashes were a potent combination any woman would find hard to resist. Emma could imagine he would be a demanding and exciting lover. She could almost feel the sexual energy emanating from him; it created a crackling tension in the air, making her feel even more on edge and hopelessly out of her depth. The thought of being legally married to him for any length of time was disturbing in the extreme. The lawyer had spoken of a marriage of convenience, but what if Rafaele wanted it to be a real marriage?

In order to pull her thoughts back into line she said the

first thing that came to her head. 'You didn't go to your father's funeral.'

'I am not one for hypocrisy,' he said, shifting his gaze from hers to sweep it over the property. 'My father would not have wanted me there, in any case. He hated me.'

Emma frowned at his embittered tone. 'I'm sure that's not true. Very few parents truly hate their children.'

His eyes came back to hers, his inherent cynicism glittering like black diamonds. 'I can only assume he thought by forcing me to marry his little nursemaid it might have some sort of reforming effect on me,' he said. 'What do you think, Miss March? Do your skills extend to taming decadent playboys?'

Emma could feel her colour rise all over again and quickly changed the subject. 'How long has it been since you were here last?' she asked.

He drew in a breath and sent his gaze back over the stately mansion. 'It has been fifteen years,' he said.

'You have lived abroad all that time?' she asked.

He turned back to look down at her. 'Yes. I've been primarily based in London but I have a couple of properties in France and Spain. But now my father is dead I intend to move back here.'

Hearing him speaking in that deep mellifluous voice of his did strange things to Emma's insides. He spoke English like a native and even had a trace of a London accent, which gave him a sophisticated air that was lethally attractive. She could imagine him travelling the globe, with a mistress in every city clamouring for his attention. He was everything a playboy should be: suave, sophisticated and utterly sexy. Even his aftershave smelt erotic—it had a citrus base and some other exotic spice that made her think of hot sultry musk-scented nights.

'Um…I have a spare set of keys for you,' she said as she led the way to the front door. 'And there's a remote control for the alarm system. I'll write down the code and password—they might have changed since you were here last.'

'I noticed you trimming the roses,' Rafaele said. 'What happened to the gardeners? Do not tell me my frugal father refused to pay them?'

Emma gave him another haughty look. 'Your father was very generous towards the staff,' she said. 'They were all provided for in his will, as I am sure you know. They are just having a couple of weeks' break. I was keeping an eye on things until you arrived.'

'What a multi-talented little nurse you are,' he said. 'I wonder what else you can turn a hand to.'

Emma fumbled through the collection of keys, conscious of his dark satirical gaze resting on her. Her heart nearly jumped out of her chest when his hand came over hers and removed the keys.

'Allow me,' he said with a glinting smile.

She stepped to one side, trying to get her breathing to even out while her fingers continued to buzz with sensation from the brief contact with his.

He opened the heavy door and waved her through with a mock bow. 'After you, Miss March.'

Emma brushed past him, her nostrils flaring again as she caught the alluring grace notes of his aftershave as they drifted towards her. She watched as he came in, his coolly indifferent gaze moving over the black and white marbled foyer with its priceless statues and paintings.

'It's a very beautiful villa,' she said to fill the echoing silence. 'You must have enjoyed holidaying here with all this space.'

He gave her an unreadable look. 'A residence can be too big and too grand, Miss March.'

Emma felt a shiver run over her bare arms that had nothing

to do with the temperature. Something about his demeanour had subtly changed. His eyes had hardened once more and the line to his mouth was grim as he looked up at the various portraits hanging on the walls.

'You are very like your father as a younger man,' she said, glancing at the portrait of Valentino Fiorenza hanging in pride of place.

Rafaele turned his head to look at her. 'I am not sure my father would have liked to be informed of that.'

'Why?' Emma asked, frowning slightly as she looked up at him.

'Did he not tell you?' he said with an embittered look. 'I was the son who had deeply disappointed him, the black sheep who brought shame and disgrace on the Fiorenza name.'

Emma moistened her lips. 'No…he didn't tell me that…' she said.

He moved down the foyer and stood for a moment in front of a portrait of a young woman with black hair and startling eyes that were black as ink. Emma knew it was his mother, for she had asked Lucia, the housekeeper. Gabriela Fiorenza had died of an infection at the age of twenty-seven when Rafaele was six and his younger brother four.

'She was very beautiful,' Emma said into the almost painful silence.

'Yes,' Rafaele said turning to look at her again, his expression now inscrutable. 'She was.'

Emma shifted her weight from foot to foot. 'Um…would you like me to make you a coffee or tea before I go?' she asked. 'The housekeeper is on leave, but I know my way around the kitchen.'

'You are quite the little organiser, aren't you, Emma March?' he asked with another one of his sardonic smiles. 'It seems even the staff are taking orders off you, taking leave at your say-so.'

She pulled her mouth tight. 'The staff are entitled to some time off. Besides, someone had to take charge in the absence of Signore Fiorenza's only son, who, one would have thought, could have at least made an effort to see him just once before he died.'

His expression became stony. 'I can see what you have been up to, Miss March. You thought you could secure yourself a fortune by bad-mouthing me to my father at every opportunity. It did not work, though, did it? You cannot have any of it without marrying me.'

Emma was finding it hard to control her normally even temper. 'I told you I had no idea what your father was up to,' she said. 'I was as shocked as you. I'm still shocked.'

He gave a little snort of disbelief. 'I can just imagine you having little heart-to-hearts with the old man, telling him how shameful it was his son refused to have any contact with him. I wonder did he tell you why, hmm? Did he allow any skeletons out of the tightly locked Fiorenza closet?'

Emma swallowed thickly. 'He...he never told me anything about you. I got the feeling he didn't like discussing the past.'

'Yes, well, that makes sense,' he said with an embittered expression. 'My father's philosophy was to ignore things he did not like facing in the hope they would eventually disappear.'

'Why *did* you leave?'

'Miss March,' he said, his look now condescending, 'I am not prepared to discuss such personal details with the hired help, even if you were elevated to the position of my father's mistress.'

'I was not your father's mistress,' Emma said crossly.

'I find that very hard to believe,' he said with another raking glance. 'You see, prior to arriving I did a little check on you, Emma Annabelle March.'

Emma's eyes widened. 'W-what?'

'I have a contact in the private-eye business,' he said, his hawk-like gaze locked on hers. 'This is not the first time a client of yours has left you something, is it?'

She moistened her lips with a nervous dart of her tongue. 'No, it's not, but I never asked for anything, not from anyone. I have had one or two clients who have left me small gifts but only because they wanted to show their appreciation. Nursing someone in the last weeks or months of their life can sometimes blur the boundaries for the patient. They begin to look upon you as a trusted friend and confidante.'

'All the same, such gifts must be quite a windfall to a girl from the wrong side of the tracks,' he went on smoothly.

'Not all people are born with a silver spoon in their mouth, Signore Fiorenza,' she said with a cold, hard stare. 'I have had to work hard to achieve what I've achieved.'

His dark, impenetrable gaze was still drilling into hers. 'According to my source you left your last client's house in a storm of controversy. Do you want to tell me about that or shall I tell you what I found out?'

Emma compressed her lips momentarily. 'I was accused of stealing a family heirloom and a large sum of money,' she said. 'I have reason to believe I was framed by a relative. The police investigating eventually agreed and the charges were dropped. In spite of my name being cleared the press were like jackals for weeks later, no doubt fuelled by the rumour-mongering of Mrs Bennett's family.'

'Is that why you moved to Italy from Australia?' he asked, his expression giving no clue as to whether he believed her explanation or not.

'Yes,' Emma said. 'I had wanted to work abroad in any case, but the Melbourne papers just wouldn't let it go. It made it hard for me to find a new placement locally. I had no choice but to start again elsewhere.'

'How did you get into this line of work?' he asked.

'I trained as a nurse but I found working in hospitals frustrating,' she said, trying to make him see that she was genuine, not the gold-digger he assumed she was. 'There was never enough time to spend with patients doing the things nurses used to do. Back rubs, sitting with them over a cup of tea, that sort of thing rarely happens these days. I started working for a private home-based care agency and really loved it. The hours can be long, of course, and it can be disruptive to one's social life when a client needs you to live in, but the positives far outweigh the negatives.'

'I am very sure they do,' he said with another mocking tilt of his lips. 'Inheriting half a luxury Italian villa and a generous allowance are hardly to be considered some of the downsides of the job.'

'Look,' Emma said on an expelled breath of irritation, 'I realise this is a difficult time for you, Signore Fiorenza. You have just lost your father and in spite of your feelings towards him that is a big thing in anyone's life, particularly a man's. I am prepared to make allowances for your inappropriate suggestions given you had no recent contact with him, but let me assure you I have nothing to hide. Your father was a difficult man, but I grew very fond of him. He was lonely and desperately unhappy. I like to think I gave him a small measure of comfort in those last months of his life.'

He stood looking down at her for a long moment before speaking. 'Let us go into the library. I would like to discuss with you how we are to handle this situation my father has placed us in.'

Emma felt her insides quiver at the look of determination in his eyes. 'There's nothing to discuss,' she said with a hitch of her chin. 'I'm going upstairs right now to pack.'

His eyes burned into hers. 'So you do not want what my father intended for you to have?'

She flicked her tongue across her suddenly bone-dry lips. 'It was very generous of him but I'm not interested in marrying for money.'

'Do you really think I am going to allow you to sabotage my inheritance?' he asked with a steely look.

Emma swallowed tightly. 'You surely don't expect me to agree to…to…marrying you…'

'I am not going to give you a choice, Miss March,' he said with implacable force. 'We will marry within a week. I have already seen to the licence. I did that as soon as I was informed of the terms of the will.'

Emma glared at him even though her heart was hammering with alarm. 'You can't force me to marry you,' she said, hoping it was somehow true.

His dark eyes glinted. 'You think not?'

I hope not, she thought as her stomach did a flip-flop of panic.

'Miss March,' he went on before she could get her voice to work. 'You will comply with the terms of the will or I will personally see to it you never work as a nurse in this country again.'

Emma sent him a defiant glare. 'I am not going to be threatened by you,' she said. 'Anyway, even if you did manage to sully my reputation in Italy I can always find work in another country. There is a shortage of nurses and carers worldwide.'

His lips thinned into a smile that was as menacing as it was mocking. 'Ah, yes, but then working as a nurse or carer you will not receive anything like the wage I am prepared to pay you to be my wife.'

Emma felt her defiant stance start to wobble. 'A…a wage?'

'Yes, Miss March,' he said with an imperious look. 'I will pay you handsomely for the privilege of bearing my name for a year.'

'How much?' she asked, and almost fell over when he told her an amount that no nurse, even if she worked for two life-times, would ever earn.

'Of course it will not be a real marriage,' he said. 'I already have a mistress.'

Emma wasn't sure why his statement should have made her feel so annoyed. She disliked him intensely, but somehow the thought of him continuing his affair with someone else while formally married to her was infuriating. 'I hope the same liberty will be open for me,' she said with a jut of her chin.

'No, Miss March, I am afraid not,' he said. 'I am a high-profile person and do not wish to be made a laughing stock amongst my colleagues and friends by the sexual proclivities of my wife.'

Emma glared at him in outrage. 'That's completely unfair! If you're going to publicly cavort with your mistress, then I insist on the same liberty to conduct my own affairs.'

His mouth tightened into a flat line. 'I will be discreet at all times, but I cannot be certain you will do the same. The way you conducted your affair with my father is a case in point. You lapped up the press attention whenever you could, hanging off him like a limpet when all the time all you wanted was his money.'

Emma clenched her teeth. 'I did *not* have an affair with your father. You can ask the household staff. They will vouch for me.'

His lip curled in scorn. 'You very conveniently sent them all off on leave, did you not?' he said. 'But even if they were here I am sure you would have convinced them to portray you as an innocent.'

She gave him a blistering glare. 'You're totally wrong about me, Signore Fiorenza, but I am not going to waste my time trying to convince you. You're obviously too cynical to be able to see who is genuine and who is not. Do you know something? I actually feel sorry for you. You are going to end up like your father, dying with just the hired help to grieve your passing.'

He ignored her comment to say, 'I expect you to act the role of a loving wife when we are within earshot or sight of other people, and that includes the household staff.'

Emma could feel her panic rising. 'But I haven't said I would marry you. I need some time to think about this.'

He looked at her for a long moment, his dark eyes quietly scanning her features. 'All right,' he said. 'I will give you until tomorrow, but that is all. The sooner this marriage starts, the sooner it ends.'

'I couldn't have put it better myself,' Emma muttered under her breath as he walked off down the long wide corridor until he finally disappeared from sight.

CHAPTER TWO

EMMA didn't see Rafaele again until later in the day. She was picking up the fallen petals from a vase of fragrant roses in the library when he sauntered in. He had changed into blue denim jeans and a close-fitting white T-shirt, which highlighted his flat stomach and gym-toned chest and shoulders. His hair was still damp from his recent shower and his jaw cleanly shaven. He looked tired however; she could see the dark bruise-like shadows beneath his eyes and the faint lines of strain bracketing his mouth.

For the first time Emma started to think about his angle on things. This magnificent villa was his heritage; it had been in the Fiorenza family for generations. No wonder he was angry at how his father had orchestrated things. Forcing him to marry a perfect stranger in order to claim what should have been rightly his would be enough to enrage anyone.

But why had Valentino chosen *her* to be his son's bride? Emma had talked to him on one or two occasions about her difficult childhood, and how she wanted one day soon to settle down with a man she loved and have a little family of her own, to have the security she had missed out on as a child. That was when he had—she had thought jokingly—suggested she marry his wealthy, successful son and fill the villa with

Fiorenza babies. It was one of the few times he had mentioned Rafaele's name. She had tried on several occasions to get him to talk about his son but he had remained tight-lipped, and, sensing the subject was painful to him, Emma had decided it was better left well alone.

'I have made a start on some dinner,' she said. 'I wasn't sure what your plans were so I made enough for two.'

He gave her a sardonic smile. 'Are you rehearsing the role of devoted wife for our temporary marriage?'

'You can interpret it any way you like, but the truth is I was merely trying to be helpful,' she said, a little stung by his attitude when she had made an effort to understand his point of view.

He held her gaze for several heartbeats. 'I noticed when I was upstairs your things are in the room connected to my father's,' he said. 'If you were not sleeping with him as you claim, why did you use that particular room when there are numerous other suites you could have occupied?'

'I was planning to move out of there as soon as you informed me of your sleeping arrangements,' she said tersely. 'I wasn't sure if you would feel comfortable sleeping in the bed in which your father died.'

A shadow flickered briefly in his eyes, like the shutter of a camera opening and closing. 'Were you with him when he passed away?' he asked.

'Yes, I was,' she answered. 'He asked me to stay with him. He told me he didn't want to die alone.'

He turned and, walking over to the bank of windows, looked down at the view of the sparkling waters of the lake, his long, straight back reminding Emma of a drawbridge being pulled up on a fortress. She had seen a lot of grief in her time; it seemed as if each member of a family had a different way of expressing it. But something about Rafaele Fiorenza made her think, in spite of his obvious anger and hatred towards his father, somewhere deep inside him was a little boy who had loved him once.

'Signore Fiorenza?' she said after a long silence.

He turned and faced her, his expression giving no clue of what was going on behind the screen of his coal-black gaze. 'Rafaele will be fine,' he said with a stiff on-off smile. 'I do not think we need to stand on ceremony given the circumstances.'

'Um…I'll just go and move my things into one of the other rooms, then…' Emma said, moving towards the door.

'The Pink Suite is probably the most comfortable,' he said. 'It was my mother's favourite. She decorated it herself. It was one of the last things she did before she died. I remember helping her with the wallpaper.'

Emma turned back to look at him. His expression had softened, as if the memory of his mother had peeled off the hard layer of cynicism he usually wore. 'The housekeeper told me your mother died when you and your brother were quite young,' she said. 'That must have been very difficult for you.'

He gave her a humourless smile. 'Life goes on, eh, Emma? Death and disorder and disease happen to us all at one time or another. The trick is to pack as much enjoyment in your life before one or all of them get their claws into you.'

'Life is certainly harder on some people than others,' she responded quietly.

He came across to where she was standing and, before she could do anything to stop him, lifted her chin with the blunt end of one long, tanned finger. 'Those grey-blue eyes of yours are full of compassion,' he said. 'But then I wonder if it is for real?'

Emma could barely breathe. The pad of his thumb was now moving back and forth against the curve of her cheek, his dark mysterious gaze mesmerising as it held hers within the force field of his. She could smell the cleanness of his freshly showered skin and the citrus spice of his aftershave, a heady combination that was intoxicating. She could see the sculptured perfection of his mouth and thought again of how it would feel to have those very experienced lips imprinted on hers. She ran her tongue out over her mouth, her heart kicking like a tiny pony behind her chest wall and her stomach doing little jerky somersaults as his thighs brushed against hers.

'Is this how you worked your magic on him, sweet, shy, caring little Emma?' he asked. 'Making him so mad with lust he promised you the world?'

Emma shook herself out of her stasis and stepped back with a glowering glare. 'I-I would prefer it you would keep your hands to yourself,' she said, annoyed that her voice shook.

He smiled in that taunting way of his. 'I will keep my hands to myself if you stop looking at me like that,' he said. 'It gives me all sorts of wicked ideas.'

She frowned at him furiously. 'I'm not looking at you with anything but disgust at your insufferable behaviour. You are one of the most obnoxious men I have ever had the misfortune to meet.'

He was still smiling at her in that mocking way of his. 'Has anyone ever told you how cute you look when you are angry?'

She swung away from him, her face flaming. 'I'm going to see to dinner,' she said and, stalking out, clicked the door shut behind her.

Rafaele waited until she was well out of earshot before he let out his breath in a long, tired stream. He sent his hand through his hair and turned and looked down at his father's antique leather-topped desk. His gaze went to where a gilt-edged photograph frame was sitting next to a paperclip dispenser, but he didn't pick it up. He didn't need to turn it around and look at his younger brother's face to summon the pain.

He still carried it deep inside him…

* * *

After Emma had transferred her things to the Pink Suite she made her way back downstairs to the massive kitchen, where through one of the windows she saw Rafaele out on the lower tier of the garden. He was standing with his hands in his trouser pockets, looking out over the expanse of verdant lawn fringed by silver birch trees, their lacy leaves quivering in the faint breeze. The same light breeze was wrinkling the surface of the lap pool, and a peahen and her vociferous mate were nearby, but it looked as if Rafaele hadn't even noticed their presence.

He stood as still as a marble statue, his tall, silent figure bathed in a red and orange glow from the fingers of light thrown by the lowering sun. The Villa Fiorenza was perhaps the most tranquil setting Emma had ever seen and yet she couldn't help feeling Rafaele Fiorenza did not find it so.

She opened the French doors leading off the terrace, the sound of her footsteps on the sandstone steps bringing his head around. She saw the way his expression became instantly shuttered, as if he resented her intrusion.

'I was wondering if you would like to eat outside,' she said. 'It's a warm evening and after such a long plane journey I thought—'

'I will not be here for dinner after all,' he said in a curt tone. 'I am going out.'

Emma felt foolish for feeling disappointed and did her best to disguise it. 'That's fine. It was nothing special in any case.'

He took the set of keys hanging on a hook on the wall. 'Do not wait up,' he said. 'I might end up staying overnight in Milan.'

'Did your mistress travel with you from London?' she asked.

'No, but what she does not know will not hurt her.'

Emma knew her face was communicating her disapproval. 'So faithfulness in your relationships isn't one of your strong points, I take it?'

'I am not sure I am the settling-down type,' he said. 'I enjoy my freedom too much.'

'I thought most Italians put a high value on getting married and having a family,' she said.

'That may have been the case for previous generations, but I personally feel life is too short for the drudge of domesticity,' he said. 'I have got nothing against children, but I like the sort you can hand back after half an hour. I have no place in my life for anything else.'

'It sounds like a pretty shallow and pointless existence to me,' Emma said. 'Don't you ever get lonely?'

'No, I do not,' he said. 'I like my life the way it is. I do not want the complication of having to be responsible for someone else's emotional upkeep. The women I date know the rules and generally are quite willing to adhere to them.'

'I suppose if they don't you get rid of them, right?'

He gave her a supercilious smile. 'That is right.'

Emma pursed her mouth. 'I feel sorry for any poor woman who makes the mistake of falling in love with you.'

'Most of the woman I know fall in love with my wallet. What they feel for me has very little to do with who I am as a person. As you have probably already guessed, I am not the type to wear my heart upon my sleeve,' he said, and then with a rueful twist to his mouth added, 'Perhaps I am my father's son after all.'

'Your father liked to give the impression he was tough, but inside he was a very broken and lonely man,' Emma said. 'I could read between the lines enough to know he had some serious regrets about his life and relationships.'

'What a pity he did not communicate that to what remained of his family while he still could,' he said with an embittered set to his mouth.

'I think he would have done so if you had made the effort to come to see him,' Emma said. 'Towards the end I couldn't help feeling he was lingering against the odds on the off chance you would visit him.'

His lip curled up in a snarl. 'He could have made the first move. Why was it left to me to do so?'

'He was *dying*,' she bit out with emphasis. 'In my opinion that shifts the responsibility to those who are well. He couldn't travel; he could barely speak towards the end. What would it have cost you to call him? These days you can call someone from anywhere in the world. What would it have cost you to give a measly five minutes of your time to allow a dying man to rest in peace?'

He stabbed a finger at her, making her take an unsteady step backwards. 'You know nothing, do you hear me? *Nothing* of what it was like being my father's son. You came into my father's life horizontally. You know nothing of what passed before. You were his carer, for heaven's sake. You were paid to wipe the dribble from his chin and change the soiled sheets on his bed, not to psychoanalyse the train-wreck of his relationships.'

Emma took a shaky breath. 'I realise this is an emotionally charged time for you, but I think—'

'I do not give a toss for what you think.' He raised his voice at her this time, his dark eyes flashing with anger. 'As I see it you exploited a dying man to feather your own nest. I find it particularly repugnant to be subjected to your lectures on what constitutes appropriate behaviour from his son when you clearly have no idea of what the dynamic of our relationship was like.'

She bit her lip. 'I'm sorry…I didn't mean to… I'm sorry…'

He let out a ragged sigh as he scraped his hand through the thickness of his hair. 'Forget about it,' he said, his tone softening. 'I should not have shouted at you. I am sorry. Put it down to overwork and jet lag. God knows I did not sleep a wink on the plane.'

'It's fine…really…I understand…it's a difficult time…'

There was a small tight silence.

'I am glad you were there for him when he died,' Rafaele said in a gruff tone. 'In spite of everything I am glad someone was there…'

'He was a good man, Signore… I mean, Rafaele,' she said. 'I think deep down he was a good man who had simply lost his way.'

He gave her a somewhat rueful smile. 'I am starting to think you make a point of seeing the good in everyone, Emma March. Is that something you learnt in your training or somewhere else?'

'No one is completely bad, Rafaele. We all have our stories, the history of what makes us the people we are. I am sure your father had his. It is a shame he didn't share his with you so you could understand the demons he had to wrestle with.'

'My father was not the sort of man to share anything with his family,' he said. 'He deplored weakness in others so I cannot imagine him ever getting to the point of confessing any of his own.'

'Were you ever close to him?' Emma asked.

His expression became shuttered again. 'He was not comfortable with small children, or even older ones when it comes to that.'

'What about your younger brother?'

His eyes turned to fathomless black. 'Has anyone ever told you that you ask too many questions?'

'I'm sorry…I just thought it might help to talk about—'

'Well, it does not help, Miss March.' He cut her off brusquely. 'And in future I would appreciate it if you would refrain from putting your nose where it is not wanted. Digging up the past serves no purpose. My father is dead and I am sorry if it offends your sensibilities, but I for one could not be happier.'

Emma stood in silence as he strode out of the room, the

echo of his embittered words ringing in her ears long after his car had roared out of the villa grounds and faded into the distance.

Emma's sister Simone called again not long after Emma had gone to bed. She sat up against the pillows and listened as Simone tearfully informed her how she had tried to apply for a personal loan only to find out there was a black mark against her credit rating. On further investigation Simone had found out her ex-partner had fuelled his cocaine habit by applying for various loans, using her as guarantor. Emma had listened in horror as Simone had described a visit late at night from a loan shark Brendan had used. The man had threatened Simone and her daughter, making it more than clear that if the money was not repaid within a week there would be unpleasant repercussions.

'I don't know what to do, Emma,' Simone sobbed. 'I'm so scared. When I picked up Chelsea from school I was sure we were being followed.'

'Have you called the police?' Emma asked, her heart thumping in alarm.

'I can't do that,' Simone said. 'You know how they treated me the last time when they came looking for Brendan. They thought I was lying about not knowing where he was or that he was using drugs. They made me feel like a criminal too.'

Emma chewed at her lip. Simone had always had it tough. In the past she had been there so many times for Emma, protecting her from one or both of their parents' drug-fuelled rages until finally the authorities had stepped in and placed both girls in foster homes. And then at the age of nineteen Simone had finally found happiness with David Harrison, but he had been killed in a motorcycle accident just six weeks after Chelsea had been born.

'Listen, Simone, I have a plan.' Emma took a shaky breath

and continued, 'It turns out the man I was nursing left me quite a bit of money in his will. It might take a few days to get it to you, but if you can tell this man Brendan owes the money to that you will settle the debt, perhaps things will calm down until you get some legal advice.'

'But, Emma, it's such a lot of money,' Simone said in anguish. 'I'll never be able to repay you, even if I do manage to take Brendan to court over this. It's not as if he's ever going to have any money to pay the legal fees, let alone the debt, even if the police do manage to track him down and arrest him.'

'I don't want to be repaid, Simone. I just want you and Chelsea to be safe,' Emma insisted. 'If things go according to plan you'll have enough money to relocate to another suburb or even to another state and make a fresh start.'

'Oh, Emma, that would be a dream come true,' Simone choked. 'I hate this place. It reminds me of our childhood, living with Mum and Dad stoned out of their brains all the time. I can't believe I didn't see it in Brendan. He was always so charming and loving. How could I have got it so wrong?'

'It's not your fault, Simone,' Emma said. 'You know what drugs do to people. They turn them into someone else. You have to move on for Chelsea's sake. It's not safe for her to be in such an environment.'

'You're right,' Simone said. 'If Dave was still alive he'd be so ashamed of me for subjecting Chelsea to this.'

'Honey, don't be so hard on yourself,' Emma said. 'I know how tough things have been for you. No one should have to deal with the stuff you've had to deal with. Just be strong, this will all go away and you'll never have to worry again.'

'I don't know how to thank you,' Simone said. 'I really don't know what Chelsea and I would do without you.'

Emma felt a little guilty not telling her sister the truth about how she was going about getting the money, but she reasoned that Simone had enough to worry about for the time being. If she were to tell Simone she was about to marry a man she had only met that morning, her sister would think she had gone mad.

But then maybe I have, Emma thought as Rafaele's handsome features came to mind. She gave the pillow a thump and settled back down but it was ages before she could relax enough to sleep…

Emma's eyes sprang open as the front door slammed. She heard Rafaele move about the villa with no attempt to keep the noise down, as if he couldn't care less about disturbing her, no doubt because he considered her an interloper in his family home.

She heard the sound of a glass shattering in the lounge room downstairs and then a course expletive cut through the still night air. She waited a few minutes, listening as various cupboards and drawers were opened and slammed shut as he began hunting through the main bathroom.

'Where the hell is the first-aid kit?' Rafaele's voice roared from the foot of the sweeping staircase.

Emma threw back the covers and, reaching for her bathrobe, tied it securely around her waist and came out on the third-floor landing. 'What's wrong?' she asked, looking down at him. 'Have you cut yourself?'

He swayed slightly on his feet as he held up his right hand wrapped in a hand towel. 'Yes, I have, as a matter of fact. Want to kiss it better, pretty Emma?'

She frowned at him as she came down the stairs. 'Have you been drinking?' she asked in a reproachful tone.

He gave her a sinful smile. 'So what if I have?'

She stood three steps above him to meet him eye to eye. 'Did you drive home in this state?'

He swayed towards her, the strong fumes of brandy wafting

over her face. 'No, I caught a cab,' he said. 'Wasn't that sensible of me?'

'It's not sensible to drink to excess even if you're not planning to be behind the wheel of a car,' she said. 'Let me look at your hand.'

He held it out to her and she gently peeled back the towel to find a gash near the base of his thumb that was still oozing blood.

'Am I going to make it through the night?' he asked with one of his mocking smiles.

Emma pursed her mouth and led him by his uninjured hand to the nearest bathroom. 'Sit on the stool,' she directed sternly as she washed her hands. 'You're very lucky, as it doesn't need stitching. I'll put a Steri-Strip on it to pull the edges together.'

She located the first-aid kit and set about cleaning the wound and dressing it. But she found it almost impossible to control the slight tremor of her hands as she touched him. His shirt sleeves were rolled back, revealing strong wrists with a generous sprinkling of dark hair, a potent reminder of his virility.

She was acutely aware of his closeness, his long legs trapping her between the basin and him at one point. He was such an intensely masculine man. She could smell the musk of his skin, this close to him she could see every pinprick of stubble on his jaw, making her fingers ache to touch him there, to see if her soft skin would snag on his rougher one.

She took an unsteady breath and tried to ignore the flutter of her pulse as his dark eyes locked on hers.

'You have very soft hands,' he said. 'I wonder if that prim little mouth of yours is just as soft.'

'I guess you'll just have to keep on wondering,' Emma said, trying to move to one side.

He stood up, his left arm blocking her exit. 'How about I kiss you and find out, eh, Emma?'

Emma gave a nervous swallow, her belly doing a funny little somersault at the smouldering look in his darker-than-ink eyes. 'I don't think that would be a good idea…'

He gave her a slow, sexy smile. 'Why not?'

She unconsciously ran her tongue over her lips. 'You know why not.'

'Is there someone else?'

'No…I mean, yes, there is,' she lied, but she knew the colour storming into her cheeks was betraying her.

'You are not a very convincing liar, Emma,' he said. 'If you were involved with someone else you would not be sending me those hungry little looks all the time, now, would you?'

'I'm doing no such thing,' she said. 'I don't know what you're talking about.'

He released her hand and placed the heated warmth of his palm at the nape of her neck instead. Emma couldn't stop the little shiver that coursed like a tickling feather all the way down her spine, loosening every vertebra along the way. Her heart began pick up its pace, the thud of her pulse so heavy she was surprised he couldn't feel it leaping beneath her skin where his hand rested.

'You want to know, don't you?' he went on in that same toe-curling, sensuous drawl. 'You have done it with the father, now you want to know what it feels like to do it with the son.'

Emma's eyes flared in shock at his crude statement. 'That's not true!'

'Did he make you come?' he asked.

She tried to push at him, but if anything it brought him closer, the stirring of his body against hers sending sparks of heat coursing through her lower body. Her breasts were jammed against his chest, her stomach hollowing out at the diamond-hard glitter of his dark gaze as it drilled into hers. 'L-let me go…' she choked. 'Y-you're drunk.'

He countered her paltry escape manoeuvre by placing his injured hand in the small of her back, his left hand now buried in the curtain of her hair. 'Perhaps a little, but that will not affect my performance,' he said. 'I can make you come like you've never come before.'

In spite of her outrage Emma could feel her body betraying her. His sultry promise set her senses alight at the thought of having him deep inside her, bringing her the sort of pleasure she had so far only dreamed about. She knew it was unusual in this day and age for a woman of twenty-six to be without sexual experience, but she had never met anyone she had been attracted to enough to take that final step. Getting involved with a playboy was not something she had ever contemplated and certainly not one as ruthless and arrogant as Rafaele Fiorenza. He was undoubtedly the most attractive man she had ever encountered, but allowing herself to be seduced by him was something she was determined to avoid if at all possible. He was an inveterate heartbreaker and she would do very well to remember it.

'I don't recall reading anything in your father's will that stipulated I have to satisfy your disgusting animal urges,' she said with as much acerbity as she could. 'Now, if you don't let me go this instant I will have to resort to slapping your face.'

He grinned at her, which wasn't quite the effect she had intended. 'You are quite something when you are all fired up,' he said. 'I bet you go off like a firecracker in bed.'

She drew in a sharp little breath, her eyes flashing him a warning. 'I don't have to put up with this,' she said. 'If you don't stop this I will pack my bags first thing in the morning to make way for Ms Henning.'

A nerve twitched at the side of his mouth, his eyes hardening to narrow chips of black ice. 'Are you blackmailing me, Emma?' he asked.

Emma lifted her chin. 'You bet I am,' she said. 'And you'd better not forget it.'

He looked at her for a long pulsing moment, his palm still on the nape of her neck. Emma tried not to show how unnerved she was by his closeness, but her heart was skipping every second beat with each drawn-out second that passed.

'You would walk away from a fortune such as this just to spite me?' he asked, dropping his hand.

Emma's neck was still tingling from the touch of his fingers. 'If I have to, yes. I refuse to be treated like a tramp. I do have some measure of pride, you know.'

'I am sure you do,' he said. 'But I wonder if you are calling my bluff.'

She gave him an arch look. 'There is only one way to find out.'

He smiled again, his dark eyes twinkling. 'Are you daring me to kiss you, Emma March?'

Her eyes widened in alarm. 'Of course not!'

'I am tempted,' he said, looking down at her mouth. 'In fact, I have never been quite so tempted.'

Emma spun on her bare feet to leave, but before she could take a single step he captured one of the ties of her bathrobe and towed her into his solid warmth like a wobbly dingy being drawn towards the safe harbour of a jetty. 'Thank you for fixing my hand,' he said. 'I really appreciate it.'

Emma had to fight against the overwhelming temptation to look at his mouth. 'It's fine…I hope it doesn't get infected.'

'If it does at least I will have you on hand to mop my feverish brow, will I not?'

She tugged her bathrobe tie out of his hold and gave him a testy glare. 'I'm sure your current mistress will do a much better job than me.'

His eyes moved over her face in a leisurely fashion, his

quiet assessment of her features even more disturbing to her than his verbal taunts. 'As of earlier tonight I have dismissed her services,' he said. 'She was starting to bore me, in any case. I have no time for emotionally needy women. They are too much hard work.'

Emma wasn't sure what to say in response. She felt a pang of empathy for the woman he had discarded so cavalierly. She wondered if he had called her or texted her on his mobile, not even bothering to wait until he could speak to her face to face. Either way she couldn't help wondering if the woman had done the unthinkable and fallen in love with him. It was a sobering reminder of what she was in for if she dared to allow her own feelings to get out of control.

'It's very late,' she said. 'You should go to bed. You look exhausted.'

He cocked his head at her. 'How about you tuck me in? I am sure you are very good at it. After all, isn't that what my father paid you to do?'

'I would have looked after him without any payment,' she said, even though she knew it was going to annoy him. 'In my opinion he was worth two of you.'

A flicker of anger flashed in his dark gaze. 'Are you telling me you were in love with him?' he asked.

She held his glittering gaze with an effort. 'Everyone deserves love, Rafaele; even, dare I say, someone as odious as you.'

She gave him one last frosty look and stalked out with the sounds of his mocking laughter following her all the way upstairs.

Her gaze narrowed slightly. 'What do you mean?'

He gave another inward smile at her artifice. 'I mean that if you make the first move I will respond to it as any full-blooded man would do in the same situation.'

She gave him a condescending look. 'So any woman with a pulse will do for you—is that it?'

'You do yourself a disservice, Emma,' he said with a lazy smile. 'You are a very attractive young woman. I would be more than happy to consummate our marriage if you should require my services.'

Her cheeks pooled with angry colour. 'I am sure I will be able to survive the duration of our marriage without resorting to such a measure of desperation,' she clipped back primly.

Rafaele felt his groin kicking with anticipation. He had never felt such wild desire before. No wonder his father had agreed to give her half of his estate. Rafaele felt like offering her double what he'd already offered just to have her on her back on the floor right here and now. He had to fight not to show how she was affecting him. He schooled his features into indifference and reached for his coffee again. 'I will have some legal papers for you to sign later today,' he said.

'What do I need to sign?' she asked with a guarded look.

'A pre-nuptial agreement, for one thing,' he said. 'I am not going to be stripped of half of my assets when we terminate our marriage.'

'How soon do I get the money you offered?' she asked.

He held her grey-blue gaze. 'How soon do you want it?'

She lowered her eyes. 'I have some debts to see to…they're rather urgent.'

'If you give me your bank account details I will see to it the moment we get back from the church.'

Her eyes flew back to his. '*The church?* You mean we're getting married in a church?'

'Do you have a problem with that?'

She sank her teeth into her lower lip for a moment. 'No… it's just I thought a register office would be more appropriate under the circumstances.'

'I do not think our marriage would be considered authentic if we did not have it consecrated by the church,' he said. 'I will also arrange for a dress and veil for you.'

'You don't have to do that.'

'It is no bother,' he said. 'My mother's wedding dress and veil have been well preserved and you are much the same size as she was.'

Her eyes were wide grey-blue pools. 'I can't wear your mother's dress!'

'Why not? People will think it a loving gesture on your part,' he said. 'Besides, this is probably going to be the only time I marry anyone so I might as well do it properly.'

Emma chewed at her bottom lip in agitation. This was going to be much harder than she had expected. Somehow she had thought a quick civil service would make her feel less married. That was vitally important to her. She didn't want to *feel* married to him.

'I will get my mother's rings out of the safe for you,' he said. 'But of course they must be returned to me once our marriage ends.'

'Yes, of course…' she said. 'I wouldn't dream of keeping them.'

'The wedding will take place tomorrow.'

Emma's heart gave a sickening lurch. 'T-tomorrow?'

'Yes,' he said. 'The legalities will be seen to this afternoon. The ceremony will take place tomorrow at the Basilica of Saint Abbondio, the ancient cathedral in the town. Have you by any chance been there?'

'I haven't done a lot of sightseeing yet,' she said. 'I was too busy looking after your father.'

He paused for a moment, his eyes still holding hers before he continued. 'We will have a small reception at a function centre afterwards, but there will of course be no honeymoon.'

'I wasn't expecting one, I can assure you,' she said. 'Besides, I need to contact the agency in regards to finding a local placement.'

'You will not be returning to the agency while you are married to me,' he said.

Emma blinked once or twice. 'What did you say?'

His dark eyes challenged hers. 'I said you will not be returning to work. I have already contacted the agency and terminated your contract.'

Emma gaped at him. 'You did *what*?'

'You are now employed by me to act as my wife. I do not want people speculating on whether this marriage is the real deal or not. What if a client needed you to live in for weeks on end? No one would expect any wife of mine to be employed and certainly not as a carer.'

'Well, no husband of mine would ever expect me to give up the job I love to pander to his needs,' Emma tossed back.

'I am not asking you to pander to my needs, but if you feel the need to do so I will not stop you.'

She gave him a blistering glare. 'What am I supposed to do all day? Laze about the pool and paint my nails? I'll go stark staring mad.'

'Think of it as a holiday, Emma,' he said. 'You can explore a hobby or two. Most of the women I know would give anything for a year to indulge themselves at a rich man's expense.'

'You really need to widen your circle of women friends,' Emma said in a crisp tone. 'Most of the women I know value their self-respect and independence too much to be indulged like a spoilt child.'

'I am sure you will adapt very quickly,' he said. 'After all, you have had plenty of practice while living with my father as your sugar daddy. Money is your motive and always has been, has it not? Why else would you be marrying me if it was not for the money?'

Emma ground her teeth. 'I don't want the money for myself,' she said. 'Otherwise I wouldn't dream of agreeing to any of this. Do you think I want to be married to someone as loathsome as you?'

A muscle leapt in his jaw. 'Careful, Emma,' he warned. 'I will not tolerate insults from you once we are married.'

Her chin came up at a defiant angle. 'If you insult me I will insult you straight back.'

His eyes glinted. 'I will enjoy taming you, Emma March,' he said. 'You are a little wildcat under that demure façade, are you not? I can see the passion in your eyes; they flash with it like twin flames of grey and blue.'

Emma felt her stomach go hollow at the sensual threat behind his statement. Her heart was suddenly racing, her skin prickling all over and her face hot with colour. If it weren't for Simone and Chelsea, she would tell him right here and now where he could put his money and his villa. But then how many times had her sister stood in the line of fire for her? Simone had taken many a slap intended for Emma; she had even had her arm broken once when she had blocked their father from lashing out at her in a fit of rage. It was not going to be easy, but surely Emma owed her sister this chance. Rafaele might not be Emma's choice of husband material, but at least it was only a temporary arrangement.

She gave him a flinty look and moved past him to pour a cup of coffee. It annoyed her to see her hand shaking as she did so, but she comforted herself that her back was turned towards him so he couldn't see.

'The lawyer will be here at three p.m.,' Rafaele said. 'In the meantime I have some work to see to in my study. If there is anything else you need for tomorrow let me know and I will see to it that you have it.'

She cradled her coffee-cup in both of her hands as she looked at him. 'Thank you but, no, there's nothing I need.'

'What about your friends?' he asked. 'Is there anyone you would like to attend the ceremony?'

'No,' she said. 'Most of my friends are in Australia. I have a couple of new acquaintances I made while I was living in Milan but no one here.'

'What about your family?' he asked. 'Obviously it is too short a notice to get them here for the wedding, but have you told them?'

She shook her head. 'There's only my sister and my niece, but I didn't want to worry them.'

He frowned at her. 'What do you mean?'

She gave him a level stare. 'My sister has always been very protective of me,' she said. 'If I told her I was marrying a virtual stranger she would have a blue fit.'

Rafaele rubbed at his jaw for a moment. 'What if she finds out some other way? An announcement or photo in the press, for instance?'

She sank her teeth into her bottom lip as she put her coffee-cup back on the counter. 'I hadn't thought about that…'

'I have been doing some thinking,' he said. 'To give our marriage some sort of credibility we shall have to tell anyone who asks we met when you first began to look after my father and up until now we have conducted a long-distance relationship.'

'Do you think that will work?' she asked.

'It will have to work. I do not want the world to know I have been manipulated into a loveless marriage by my father's machinations from the grave.'

'I'm not going to lie to my sister,' she said with a spark of defiance in her eyes.

'As far as I see it you have already done so by omission,' he pointed out. 'Concealing the truth is the same as lying in my book.'

She gave him an arch look. 'And yet you are prepared to lie to the world about your relationship with me.'

'I am prepared to compromise quite a few of my standards in order to secure what is rightly mine, including sleeping with the enemy if she so desires.'

Her eyes flashed at him again. 'This particular enemy has no such desire.'

He smiled and stepped closer, close enough to take her chin between his index finger and thumb. 'Are you prepared to lay some money down on that, Emma?' he asked in a silky tone.

He felt her tremble under his touch and his groin leapt in response. Her mouth was like a soft, plump cushion of pink flesh just begging to be kissed. The more he thought about it, the more he wanted to do it. He lowered his head, slowly, watching as her eyes widened before her lashes began to come down, her lips parting slightly, her sweet breath mingling with his, giving him all the invitation he needed.

Emma came to her senses just in time. She slipped out of his light hold, her heart hammering, her breath catching and her senses on fire. 'What the hell do you think you're doing?' she said, rubbing at her chin as if he had burnt her.

'I was doing what you were all but begging me to do,' he answered smoothly.

She glared at him. 'I was doing nothing of the sort. You touched me. I didn't touch you.'

'You will have to touch me tomorrow. In fact you will have to kiss me in front of the congregation, so perhaps we should rehearse it a couple of times now.'

Emma couldn't quite control the flutter of nerves in her belly. 'I-I don't think that will be necessary,' she faltered. 'Surely we can just…you know…wing it at the time…'

He gave a wry smile. 'Wing it?'

'Ad lib,' she said. 'You know…go on instinct…'

His eyes darkened to black pools of ink. 'I thought that was exactly what I was just doing,' he said, 'and so were you if you were honest with yourself.'

'Maybe I was thinking of your father,' she said, even though she knew it would infuriate him. Better that than admit to him how much she had wanted him to kiss her. That was just asking too much of her pride, battered as it was.

His features went tight with anger. 'You gold-digging little whore,' he bit out savagely. 'I swear to God you will not be thinking of my father when I finally take you to my bed.'

His confidence fuelled Emma's defiance. She gave her head a little toss and gave him a taunting look. 'That is not part of the deal, Rafaele, remember? If you want the goods on display, then you will have to pay extra for them.'

A nerve pulsed like a jackhammer at the side of his mouth. 'Goddamn you,' he ground out. 'I am not paying another penny for a cheap little tramp like you. When you come to me you will do so because you want it so badly you cannot help yourself.'

Emma stood her ground as he brushed past her in a swish of anger-filled air that lifted the strands of hair about her face. She closed her eyes once the door clicked shut behind him, her chest deflating on an expelled breath, her throat tight with the effort of holding back a stray and totally unexpected sob.

* * *

Emma heard the lawyer arrive just on three in the afternoon and made her way downstairs to the library. She wished she had thought to ask Rafaele what he intended to tell his legal advisor about their relationship. As she came into the room she looked at him for guidance but his expression was impenetrable.

Brief introductions were made and she sat down and began reading through the wordy documents, deliberately taking her time before she signed the places marked with a sign-here sticker. Emma had no problem with signing a pre-nuptial agreement—several of her friends back home in Australia had done so when they had begun living with their partners or got married. She totally understood Rafaele's position, he couldn't risk a division of his assets upon their inevitable divorce, but somehow she wished things were different between them. She wasn't used to people taking an instant dislike to her. Even her parents, for all their faults, had not really hated her; they had just loved their drugs more.

She signed the last place and gave the lawyer a smile. 'Thank you for going to the trouble of printing a copy for me in English.'

'Prego.'

Once the lawyer had left Rafaele turned to Emma. 'I have left my mother's dress and veil in the dressing room upstairs. If it is not suitable will you let me know immediately so I can come up with an alternative?'

Emma arched her brows at him. 'You must have some very fancy connections in that little black book of yours if you can come up with wedding finery at short notice.'

'There are certain advantages in being extremely wealthy,' he returned with a stretch of his lips that was almost, but not quite, a smile.

'Yes, well, you're lucky, I suppose, that you've got that going for you in compensation for your other numerous short-comings,' she said with a pert tilt of her chin.

'If you are looking for an apology for this afternoon's discussion I am not going to give it to you,' he said.

'I wasn't expecting you to be civil,' she threw back. 'I know that about you at the very least.'

His black-brown gaze clashed with hers. 'You will know a whole lot more about me before this marriage is over, let me assure you.'

She gave a bored sigh and folded her arms across her chest. 'I can hardly wait.'

Rafaele felt his control slipping. She was goading him deliberately, making him feel things he didn't want to feel. He had never met a more infuriating woman, or a more desirable one. He wanted her so badly his body burned with it. The blood was already thick and heavy in his groin, the pulse of lust so strong he could feel it pounding in his ears. But acting on it was out of the question, or at least until they were officially married. She stood between him and his last link with his father. If he made a wrong move now she might pull the plug just to spite him. How could he trust her? For all he knew she might have cooked this scheme up with that cold-hearted bitch Sondra Henning. They could share the spoils of their victory, leaving him with nothing.

He was *not* going to let that happen.

He rearranged his features and forced his tense shoulders to relax. 'This is not getting us anywhere,' he said. 'We are arguing like children in a playground. Tomorrow is going to be difficult enough for both of us.'

'I couldn't agree more,' she said. 'That is why I am going to have an early night. If you want dinner you will have to make it yourself.'

Rafaele frowned at her churlish expression. 'I do not expect you to prepare my meals, Emma. That is what I have a housekeeper for. I have employed a temporary one to fill in until my father's lady returns from leave. She will start next week. I could not get anyone any sooner.'

'Have you told her our marriage is not a real one?'

'I did not see the necessity to do so,' he said.

'Isn't she going to think it rather unusual we will not be sharing a bedroom?'

'Many couples do not share a bedroom for a variety of reasons,' he said. 'I will tell her I am a very light sleeper if you like.'

'Fine,' she said and turned to leave.

'Emma?'

He heard her draw in a breath of petulance as she turned back to face him. 'Yes?'

He searched her features for a beat or two. 'I hope I do not need to remind you that I expect you to refrain from bringing any of your lovers back here to the villa.'

She arched her brows at him. 'Do I get the same guarantee from you?'

'Any affairs I conduct will be discreet.'

Her eyes flashed with sparks of grey-blue hatred. 'If you embarrass me publicly, then I swear to God I will do the same to you.'

Rafaele held her feisty glare. 'Do so at your peril, Emma. You might think you have got the upper hand now your goal of marrying a rich man is just hours away, but do not forget who you are dealing with. My father might have been a weak-willed pushover, but you will not find me so easy to manipulate. You put one foot out of line and you will live to regret it. I will make sure of it.'

She gave him an insolent look. 'Do you have any idea how much I loathe and detest you?'

His mouth tilted in a mocking smile. 'If it is even half of

what I feel for you, then I would say we are in for a very entertaining year of marriage.'

'I am not staying married to you any longer than necessary,' she said with another defiant glare. 'Once I have what I want I am leaving.'

'Believe me, Emma Money-Hungry March,' he drawled dryly, 'I will be the first on hand to help you pack your bags.'

She looked as if she was going to fling another retort his way, but suddenly seemed to change her mind. Instead she pressed her lips tightly together and brushed past him, her gait stiff with haughtiness. It was only later, much later, that he recalled seeing a glisten of moisture in her eyes before she had lowered them out of the reach of his.

CHAPTER FOUR

WHEN Emma came downstairs the following morning wearing the wedding dress and veil Rafaele's mother had worn on her wedding day he felt a shock wave of reaction go through him. She had styled her chestnut hair into a smooth princess-like chignon at the back of her head, her flawless face lightly made up with foundation and eye-shadow and just a hint of blusher on her cheeks. Her lips were a glossy pink and the fragrance she wore floated down towards him with every cautious step she took as the dress's train followed her down the stairs.

He felt his throat go dry and had to swallow a couple of times to clear it enough to speak. 'You look very beautiful, Emma,' he said. 'I have never seen a more stunning bride.'

'I feel like a dreadful fraud,' she said with a little downturn of her mouth.

He took her by the elbow and led her out to where his car and driver were waiting. 'This is going to be the easy part. The priest tells us what to say and we say it. You have probably been to or seen enough weddings on television to know how to act. Just smile constantly and look adoringly at me.'

She gave him a surly look without responding.

He settled her into the limousine and took the seat beside

her, holding her hand in his. 'Stop frowning, Emma,' he said. 'Think about the money that is going to be in your bank account at the end of today. Surely that should bring a smile to any woman's face.'

She turned her head away to look out of the window. 'I can't wait for this to be over,' she said.

Rafaele felt the slight tremble of her fingers where they were resting against his. He gave her hand a little squeeze. 'Do not worry, Emma, it soon will be.'

The ceremony was very traditional even if the bride and groom had arrived in the same car, Emma thought as she mechanically repeated her vows. Then the moment came when the priest instructed the groom to kiss his bride. Emma could feel the anticipation of the congregation as Rafaele gently lifted the veil off her face. Her breathing came to a jerky halt in her chest as his eyes locked on hers. Her heart began to thud as he brought his head down, his warm, mint-fresh breath caressing the surface of her lips before he pressed his against them in a kiss that went from feather-light to red-hot passion within a heartbeat. Sensation exploded inside her as his tongue slipped through the softly parted shield of her lips to mate with hers in a blatant act of possession that sent electric shivers up and down her spine. Her breasts tightened and tingled simultaneously, her legs trembling so much she could barely stand upright and would have melted in a pool at Rafaele's feet if his hand hadn't been pressed to the small of her back, holding her against his rock-hard body. She felt the stirring of his groin against her, making her even more acutely aware of the formal ties that now bound them.

When he finally lifted his mouth off hers, Emma gave a tremulous smile for the benefit of the congregation, or at least that was what she told herself at the time. Rafaele smiled back, a warm, generous smile that made his eyes go very dark and the lines about his mouth relax, making him look all the more irresistibly handsome.

After the register was signed Emma stood sipping a glass of champagne an hour or so later, smiling until her face ached as she was introduced to the various colleagues and friends Rafaele had invited at short notice. Numerous people raved about her dress, remarking how it had made the wedding all the more special to think she had worn it in honour of Rafaele's much-loved mother.

One woman in particular, someone who had known Gabriela Fiorenza personally, came and spoke to Emma while Rafaele was engaged in a conversation elsewhere. 'I am so very glad Rafaele has found someone like you,' she said in heavily accented English. 'He always said he would never fall in love and marry, but that is because he did not want to end up like his father. Valentino did not handle Gabriela's death very well. He had been in love with her practically since childhood. And then losing poor Giovanni…' The woman crossed herself. 'God rest his soul.'

Emma wanted to ask what had happened to Rafaele's younger brother, but realised it might appear strange if she did so. As his bride she would be expected to know everything there was to know about Rafaele and his family, but, she realised with an unnerving quiver deep inside her belly as she met his gaze across the room, she knew very little…

Once the official photographs were taken and the wedding cake cut, Rafaele led her out to the car where the driver transported them back to the villa.

He turned to her once they were inside. 'I will leave you to get changed. It has been a long day. I will see to the electronic transfer of the funds I promised you, also I have some stocks and shares to look up on my computer, which may take some time, so if you will excuse me, I will say good-night.'

'Rafaele?'

His expression locked her out. 'The money is yours, Emma,' he said. 'That is what you wanted, was it not?'

She rolled her lips together, her eyes falling away from his. 'Yes…' she said. 'Yes, it is…'

'I will see you in the morning.'

Emma lifted her gaze, but he was already striding away down the hall towards the study as if he couldn't wait to get away from her.

Emma barely caught sight of Rafaele during the next couple of days. He came in late at night and left before she was up in the morning, which should have made her feel relieved but somehow didn't.

She did, however, get some measure of comfort from transferring Simone the funds to clear away the debt. She even decided to come clean and tell her sister about her marriage to Rafaele in case it was reported in the press back in Melbourne. Simone was shocked and expressed her concern about Emma marrying a man she barely knew, but Emma tried to reassure her by pointing out Valentino Fiorenza would never have insisted on such a scheme if he had not trusted his son to do the right thing by her.

'You're not going to do something stupid like fall in love with this man, are you, Emma?' Simone asked.

'Of course not!' Emma laughed off the suggestion but later, after she had ended the call, she wondered if she had tempted fate by being quite so adamant. She could still feel the imprint of his lips on hers and her belly gave a little twitch-like movement every time she thought of his tongue moving against hers.

The last thing she wanted to do was to develop feelings for Rafaele, but as she moved about the property she couldn't help thinking what it must have been like for him and his younger brother growing up without a mother. Every time she walked through the villa or gardens she imagined two little bewildered boys wandering around the huge mansion and grounds without the comfort and nurture of their mother. In many ways it reminded her of her own childhood, but at least she had had Simone to turn to. But then that also brought it home to her how lonely Rafaele's childhood must have been after the death of his younger brother Giovanni. Rafaele had only been ten years old at the time. The large rooms, though beautiful, were formal and rather ostentatious, the many priceless paintings and objets d'art clearly not conducive to the presence of a young child.

As she had guessed, Rafaele had chosen not to occupy his father's suite and instead had placed his things in one of the suites on the third level. For days Emma had felt uncomfortable even walking past his private domain, although she felt inexplicably drawn to the room every time she walked past to her own suite further along the hall. Finally she could stand it no longer, and, once she was confident she was alone in the villa, she opened the door and went in.

The huge bed was neatly made and several books were sitting on the bedside table, all but one of them in English. She could smell the trace of citrus in his aftershave lingering in the air and her nostrils automatically flared to take more of it in.

The sunlight slanted in at the windows, the dust motes rising like tiny wraiths in the air. Before she was even aware of what she was doing Emma moved across the room to sit on the bed, the creak of protesting springs sounding like a warning in the silence. She ran her hand over the pillow, smoothing out the indentation where his head had lain the night before.

She wondered if this had been his room while growing up at The Villa Fiorenza, but if it had been it held no trace of his previous occupation. His brother's room on the nursery floor, on the other hand, was like a shrine. When she had gone in there for the first time a few days ago she had been more than a little taken aback to find the wardrobe still contained his clothes; his shoes were still lying at the bottom with his socks stuffed inside as if at any moment he were coming back to claim them. His toys and junior soccer trophies lined every available surface and, even more disturbingly, the urn with his ashes held pride of place on the mantel above the fireplace. Emma had found it a little creepy being in there. She felt as if the house wasn't quite ready to let Giovanni Fiorenza leave even though, according to the inscription on the urn, he had died twenty-three years ago.

She looked at the photograph hanging on the wall; Giovanni had been as dark as his brother with the same deep brown eyes, but there was a relaxed and friendly openness about his features that wasn't present in his brooding older brother's. The photograph portrayed Rafaele as a rather serious young boy who looked as if he were carrying the weight of the world upon his thin shoulders.

Even though Emma had been in every room in the villa by now she had seen not a single photograph of Rafaele in the years since his brother had died.

She couldn't help wondering why.

Emma was in the salon falling asleep over a book the following evening when Rafaele came into the room. She put the book to one side and got to her feet, suddenly feeling uncomfortable in case he somehow sensed where she had been mooching around earlier.

'That looks like a riveting read,' he remarked dryly.

She gave him a sheepish look. 'I guess I must be a little tired. I should have been in bed an hour ago.'

His brow creased slightly. 'I hope you are not overdoing things,' he said. 'I noticed you have taken all the covers off the furniture in the spare rooms. Surely that can wait until the new housekeeper starts in a day or so?'

'I thought the place needed airing,' Emma said. 'Some of those rooms look like they have been shut for years.'

He studied her for a moment. 'What are you up to, Emma? Making an inventory of all the valuables for when we finally divorce?'

'I am merely trying to make this place habitable,' she said, frowning at him crossly. 'It's a huge villa and too much work for one housekeeper. I don't know how Lucia had managed for as long as she has. No wonder she wanted a break.'

He held her fiery look for a tense moment. 'Were you waiting up for me, Emma?' he asked.

'No, of course I wasn't,' she said, annoyed with herself for the creep of colour she could feel staining her cheeks. He was so worldly and in control while she always felt so flustered and out of her depth in his presence.

'Actually, I am glad you are still up,' he said. 'Do you fancy a nightcap?'

'Um…OK…'

'What would you like to drink?' he asked, turning to the well-stocked drinks cabinet.

'A small sweet sherry…if you have it,' she said.

He poured himself a cognac after he'd handed her the sherry and came and sat beside her on the sofa, touching his glass briefly against hers. '*Salute.*'

'*Salute,*' Emma said and took a tiny sip.

'I thought only grey-haired Sunday-school teachers drank that stuff,' he said with a crooked smile.

Emma felt a little stung at what she perceived was a criticism. 'I suppose I must seem terribly unsophisticated to someone like you.'

'On the contrary, I find you rather intriguing.'

'I thought you said I was a money-hungry slut who was intent on making herself a fortune, or words to that effect,' she returned with a tart edge to her tone.

'I may have been a little hasty in my judgement,' he acceded. 'Although I guess only time will tell.'

'You can't quite accept there are still people in the world who genuinely care about others, can you?' she asked.

'You were being *paid* to care, Emma,' he pointed out. 'My father obviously did not know the difference. He fooled himself into thinking you were worthy of half of his estate. How does it feel now you have achieved your goal?'

'I told you before I did absolutely nothing to encourage your father's decision,' she insisted.

'He only changed his will once you had come into his life,' he said. 'How did you do it, Emma? How many times did you have to crawl into his bed to sweeten him up a bit?'

'That's a disgusting thing to say,' she said.

His top lip curled. 'My father always had a thing for women young enough to be his daughter,' he said. 'He liked to show them off like a trophy. It used to sicken me to see them fawning all over him. None of them had any time for my brother and I. They were after my father's money just like you.'

Emma got to her feet. 'I don't have to listen to this.'

His flashing dark eyes raked her mercilessly. 'So how did you manage it, Emma? Could he still get it up towards the end or did you have to give him a bit of encouragement with that pretty little mouth of yours?' he asked.

Emma lifted her hand to his face, but he blocked it with

one of his, the grip of his strong fingers almost brutal around her slender wrist.

'I don't think so, *poco moglie di miniera*,' he said. 'Not unless you want to face the consequences.'

She ground her teeth as she pulled at his hold. 'It's no wonder your father stripped this house of every single photograph of you,' she said with uncharacteristic spite. 'He must have hated being reminded of the sort of person you turned out to be. I have never met a more hateful despicable man.'

His fingers tightened even further. 'Perhaps I should give you an even better reason to hate me,' he said and tugged her towards him, her breasts pressed tight to his chest. 'After all, that is what you really want me to do, is it not? You have wanted it from the start. My father cannot have been much use to a young nubile woman like you. How long has it been since you had a real man in your bed?'

Emma threw him a heated glare. 'I wouldn't dream of demeaning myself by spending even a second in yours.'

His mouth tilted mockingly. 'Now that is very interesting you should say so, for you spent a whole lot longer than that on it this afternoon, did you not, Emma?' he asked.

Her eyes widened, her voice sticking at the back of her throat. 'I-I don't know what you're talking about.'

He picked up a lock of her hair and slowly wound it round one of his fingers. 'Little liar,' he said. 'Guess what I found lying on my pillow? A couple of chestnut-brown hairs that look to me as if they came from that clever little calculating head of yours.'

Emma knew she had no real way to defend herself, but it didn't stop her trying. 'I went in there to check if you needed any washing done,' she said. 'There was nothing else to it.'

He slowly unwound her hair, his eyes holding hers like a mesmerised rabbit. 'I know what you are doing, Emma,' he said. 'You are turning up the heat, bit by bit, just like you did with my father.'

'I am doing no such thing!'

'Can you feel what you are doing to me?' he asked, pressing her closer to where his lower body was thickening. 'Feel it, Emma.'

Emma felt it and it secretly terrified her. She had never felt the overwhelming power of physical attraction quite like this before, it smouldered like red-hot coals deep inside her, making her a slave to the senses he had awakened. She wanted to feel his commanding lips on hers again; she had been dreaming of it for days. She wanted to feel the hot brand of his mouth suckling on her breasts, her stomach, her thighs and the secret heart of her that throbbed and pulsed with longing for him even now.

'Damn you, Emma,' he growled, putting her away from him roughly. 'I want you but I hate myself for it. I swore I would never touch a woman my father had slaked his lust on first.'

'I didn't have that sort of relationship with your father,' Emma said in frustration. 'Why won't you believe me?'

'Do you expect me to believe he handed over half of his estate just because you smoothed the sheets on his deathbed?' he asked. 'I am not that much of a fool.'

'There's nothing I can say to convince you otherwise, is there?' she said. 'You want to believe your father set out to deliberately thwart you, but I don't believe he did.'

His mouth twisted with scorn. 'Oh, come on now, Emma. You're surely not going to tell me he had a last-minute change of mind and told you how much he really loved me, are you?'

'Why did you hate him so much?' Emma asked.

His expression became stony and the seconds ticked by before he answered. 'I didn't like him for many reasons,' he said. 'For the first few years of my life he was everything a father should be, but after my mother died he changed. It was like living at a perpetual funeral. He would snap at my younger brother and I for the most inconsequential things. In his opinion we were meant to grieve indefinitely, but Giovanni was too young to remember much about our mother. He was just a little child who was forced to walk around on tiptoe. I could not always protect him from one of my father's outbursts.'

Emma swallowed. 'Did he…did he physically abuse your brother or you?' she asked in a hollow whisper.

His lips tightened to a thin white line. 'Oh, he was far too clever to leave marks and bruises that could raise suspicion if noticed by others,' he said. 'He liked to use other, more subtle means of control. His modus operandi was more along the lines of emotional abuse, such as the systematic erosion of self-esteem and stripping away of confidence.'

'I'm so sorry,' she said, biting her lip momentarily. 'It must have been very painful for you growing up like that.'

'It is ironic that I have achieved the sort of success I have,' he said. 'Perhaps I would not have gone so far without the harsh lessons my father subjected me to, but in spite of that I can never find it in myself to forgive him.'

'He's dead, Rafaele,' Emma said. 'What point is there in hating him now? What will it achieve? You'll only end up bitter and twisted, not to mention desperately unhappy.'

'Is that what you told him in his last days?' he asked with a mocking set to his mouth. 'Forgive and forget? Perhaps there is a little of the grey-haired Sunday-school teacher in you after all.'

'From the very first day I went to his palazzo in Milan to look after him I felt he was struggling with some issues to do with his family,' Emma said. 'Over the months I gently encouraged him to make his peace with whoever he needed to. I tell all my terminally ill clients that. I think it's very important they leave this world with some sense of closure.'

'What was his reaction?' Rafaele asked.

She gave a soft sigh, a small frown creasing her smooth brow. 'He didn't say much, but I got the impression he was thinking about it a great deal. I think he found it very painful, you know…confronting the past, but then a lot of people feel that way. I felt sorry for him. I found him crying one day not long before he died. He was inconsolable but he wouldn't tell me what had upset him.'

'Were you there the day he contacted his lawyer?'

'No, but I think it must have happened one afternoon when I had taken a couple of hours off,' she answered. 'He never mentioned anything to me about a visitor coming and neither did Lucia, the housekeeper, who often kept an eye on him for me while I was doing errands.'

Rafaele wondered whether or not to believe her. She was certainly very convincing with her soft grey-blue eyes misting slightly as if she had genuinely been fond of his father. But how could he be sure? She had made all but a token protest about marrying him in order to gain her share of the estate, and even more damning was the scandal over her previous client back in Australia. He had looked up the newspaper articles on the Internet and read the various interviews with the family members, who had each painted Emma March as an opportunist who had inveigled her way into their senile mother's affections before stealing from her. That the charges were later dropped hadn't satisfied the family, who still staunchly believed Emma to have used the old woman's dementia to throw doubt on the case.

As he saw it, Emma was either a genuinely caring person who had become the unfortunate victim of a hate campaign by jealous relatives, or she was indeed a conniving con-artist with greed as her motive.

It sickened him to think of her playing up to his father

to manipulate him into changing his will in her favour at the last hour. The thought of her firm young body being pawed over by a ruthless old man like his father churned his stomach. But then he already knew how far a woman would go for money. The mistress his father had kept after Giovanni had died, Sondra Henning, was a case in point. Thirty-odd years his father's junior she had made no effort to hide her intentions. She had been a spiteful bitch when his father wasn't looking. She had subjected Rafaele to the lash of her tongue and the slap of her hand. He couldn't bear the thought of that home-wrecker taking anything else away from him.

Emma March might be a ruthless little gold-digger, but she had a sensual aura about her that was potently seductive. She wasn't classically beautiful by any means, but there was something about her girl-next-door vitality that drew him in like a magnet. Every time he touched her he felt the electrifying voltage of her body charging into his. Her slim but femininely curvy body made him ache to feel her writhing beneath him in the throes of passion. He wanted to feel his hard, thickened body driving into the yielding softness of hers until they both exploded. He wanted to feel her primly pursed mouth sucking on him until he burst with pleasure. He wanted to taste her, to explore her tender contours and bring her to the pinnacle of fulfilment he knew she craved. He had seen it in her eyes almost from the first moment they had met. That hungry, yearning look was unmistakable.

'It has all worked out rather brilliantly for you, has it not, Emma?' he asked. 'All your hard work has paid off. Either way you win.'

She looked at him hesitantly. 'I'm not sure what you mean…'

He smiled a cynical smile. 'You have a roof over your head for the duration of our marriage and a guaranteed income at the end of it, a windfall most people would not dream of seeing in a lifetime.'

'I keep telling you I was never interested in your father's money,' she said. 'As far as I can make out he apparently wanted you to spend some time at The Villa Fiorenza and the only way he thought he could bring it about was to tie you here with me.'

Rafaele snapped his brows together. 'This villa has been in the Fiorenza family for several generations. I spent some of the happiest years of my life in this place before my mother and brother died. I will be damned if I will let one of my father's whores take even a single pebble from the driveway without my permission.'

'I'm not planning on making things unpleasant or difficult for you,' she said. 'You can live your life and I'll live mine. We don't even have to communicate with each other if we don't want to.'

'Your very presence here makes things difficult,' Rafaele muttered as he set his glass down with a loud thwack. 'But perhaps that is what you and my father planned.'

She frowned at him. 'I'm not sure what you're suggesting, but I can assure you I am finding this as difficult if not more so than you. The sooner we end this farce, the better, as far as I am concerned.' With one last searing glance, she stalked out, leaving him with just his empty glass for company.

CHAPTER FIVE

AFTER their exchange Emma did her best to avoid Rafaele, although at one point she watched him from her upstairs window as he swam lap after lap in the pool, his strong, leanly muscled body carving through the water with effortless ease. She felt a little guilty drinking in the sight of him, but she couldn't seem to drag her eyes away. His body was so wonderfully built; lean but powerful, muscular without being over-bulky. His olive skin was a deep even brown as if he had recently spent some time somewhere tropical. His black hair was like wet silk as he vaulted out of the water, the water droplets on his body glistening in the afternoon sun. As he reached for his towel he looked up and locked gazes with her, the lazy smile he sent her seeming to suggest he had known all along she was up there staring down at him.

Emma turned from the window with her heart doing little back flips in her chest, her face hot and her pulse racing out of control. She was deeply ashamed of her reaction to him. She felt like a gauche schoolgirl instead of a grown woman. He had only to look at her and she felt her colour begin to rise both inside and out. That dark smouldering gaze of his set her senses alight every time it rested on her and it seemed there was nothing she could do to stop it. It galled her to think he of all people had such an effect on her. He was an unprincipled playboy, a man who used women as playthings, discarding them when they no longer appealed to him. She knew if she was fool enough to succumb to his potent charm he would break her heart and think nothing of it. After all it would be the perfect revenge to get back at her for what he was convinced she had done to profit from his father's will.

The new housekeeper came to work at the villa each morning, along with the team of gardeners, which left Emma with even less to do to occupy her time. She caught up on some reading and went for long walks about the town, visiting some of the places she had read about in her travel guide. The tourist season was in full swing by now and she mingled with the crowds, stopping for coffee at one of the many cafes until the heat of the day brought her back to the villa.

After a few days, once the staff had left for the day Emma made the most of the warm weather by dipping in and out of the pool. The water was cool against her heated skin and she closed her eyes and floated on her back, enjoying the sounds of the garden, the birds twittering in the shrubs and trees, the gentle lap of water and the soothing tinkle of the wind chimes hanging in the arbour.

'Mind if I join you?' Rafaele's deep voice sounded from the deck of the pool.

Emma jerked upright, water shooting up her nose as she tried to find her feet. 'You scared me!' she said, blinking the water out of her eyes. 'I thought you'd gone out.'

'I did, but I have been back about an hour,' he said. 'I thought I might find you out here. How is the water?'

'It's…lovely,' she said, trying not to stare at his leanly

muscled body. He was dressed in black bathers, the close-fitting Lycra outlining his masculine form so lovingly she felt her breath hitch in her throat.

He dived in and swam several lengths, the effortless motion of his arms and legs making Emma's earlier efforts seem rather pathetic by comparison.

'Want a race to the other end?' he asked as he came up close by.

'I'm not quite in your league,' she said with a self-conscious grimace.

'Come on, Emma, be a devil,' he said. 'I will give you a head start.'

Emma took a deep breath and threw herself into it, her arms going like windmills and her feet and ankles flapping with all their might. She thought she was in with a chance until she felt one of his hands grasp her by one of her ankles and pull her backwards through the water. She came up spluttering, and as she twisted round to face him her hands somehow landed on his chest, her legs tangling with his under the water. 'You cheated!' she spluttered.

He smiled at her. 'One thing you should know about me, Emma, is I do not always play by the rules.'

She gave him a reproachful look. 'In my book you're not a winner unless you've won fair and square.'

His hands settled on her hips, his lower body brushing against hers as he kept them both afloat. 'Ah, yes, but then I make it a point of always winning,' he said, looking down at her mouth.

Emma could hardly breathe. His mouth was so close she could see the pepper of stubble on his jaw, his warm breath like a caress as he came even closer. 'D-don't…' she said in a hoarse whisper.

He lifted one brow. 'You do not want me to kiss you?'

She looked into his dark, smouldering gaze. 'I think it's best if you don't…'

'Why is that?' he asked, still holding her against him.

'Um…I think it's not wise to complicate things…'

One of his hands moved from the curve of her hip to settle at the back of her neck beneath the wet curtain of her hair. 'How will it complicate things if I kiss you?' he asked.

Emma took a tight little swallow. She knew exactly what one kiss would do. As it was she had been trying to stamp out the memory of the wedding kiss without success. 'I don't want to…to develop feelings for you, Rafaele,' she said.

His eyes searched hers for a long moment. 'You think that is likely to happen?'

'I'm not a casual hook-up type of person,' she said. 'After this…arrangement is over I want to get married and have a family. I'm twenty-six years old. I don't want to leave it too late to settle down. I want stability and commitment. You're not the person to give me those things.'

A hard light came into his eyes. 'Nor was my father, but that did not stop you from talking him into giving you a fortune.'

Emma pulled out of his hold. 'You're starting to sound like a broken record, Rafaele. I'm not even going to waste my breath denying it again.'

'Have dinner with me tonight.'

She frowned at him. 'What?'

'Let's go out for a meal,' he said. 'Let's do it the old-fashioned way. Guy meets girl, that sort of thing. Let's forget about my father and take it one step at a time.'

'Rafaele…this is crazy,' she said.

'What is so crazy about two people going out to dinner and strengthening their acquaintance?' he asked. 'After all, we have got to live together for months on end—wouldn't it be better if at the end of it we were friends instead of enemies?'

'I can't imagine us ever being friends.'

'Only because we got off to a bad start,' he said. 'I am not always such a brute you know. I can be quite charming when I put my mind to it.'

Yes, well, that's what I'm worried about, Emma thought. She was having enough trouble keeping her head as it was. God only knew what would happen to her heart if he laid on the Fiorenza charm at full strength. She had seen a glimpse of it already, that lazy smile and those dark, smouldering eyes had set her heart racing a few times too many. 'All right,' she said. 'I'll have dinner with you, but only because it's the housekeeper's afternoon off.'

He grinned at her, a boyish grin that sent her stomach into another dip-and-dive routine. 'You really know how to annihilate a man's ego, don't you?' he said.

Emma felt an answering smile tug at the corners of her mouth. 'I'm sure yours should be listed as one of the great wonders of the world,' she said. 'In fact I bet it can be seen from outer space.'

'I can see I am going to have to work extra hard to improve your opinion of me,' he said. 'But who knows what a bit of wining and dining will do? I am going to have a bit more of a swim before I get out and have a shower. Is eight-thirty OK with you?'

'Sure,' Emma said, moving to the side of the pool, her stomach already fluttering with excitement. 'I'll be ready.'

When Emma came downstairs close to eight-thirty Rafaele was waiting for her in the salon. He had been reading through one of the weekend papers and rose to his feet as she came in, his gaze running over her appreciatively. 'You look stunning, Emma,' he said, 'absolutely stunning.'

'Thank you,' Emma said shyly.

'I thought we could eat at a restaurant at Villa Olmo,' he said as he led the way out to his car. 'Have you had a chance to visit it yet?'

'No, but I've walked past it a couple of times,' she said. 'It's very grand, isn't it?'

'It's the most famous residence of Como,' he informed her. 'The villa owes its name to an elm tree that in ancient times grew inside the park. The architect was Simone Cantoni and now the town of Como owns it and uses it for various exhibits. The restaurant is situated to the right of the villa.'

'I've made a bit of a start on my sightseeing,' Emma said. 'I've been to Duomo, the cathedral, and to the Volta temple and on the Funicular so far.'

He glanced at her. 'Did you walk up to the lighthouse?'

'Yes, it was an amazing view from up there,' she said. 'I didn't want to leave.'

'The funicular has been running from the end of the eighteen hundreds,' he said. 'From the top you can make out the castrum, the rectangle that made up the old establishment of the Roman town. You can even see the first basin of the lake and the villas and plains that lead to Milan.'

Emma looked at him. 'Did you miss all this while you were living abroad?'

He took a moment to answer. 'Yes, I did miss it,' he said. 'There was many a time I wanted to come back, but it was impossible.'

'Do you really think your father would have turned you away from the door?' she asked.

His hands tightened on the wheel, the only sign Emma could see of his tension. 'When I left fifteen years ago he made it quite clear I would not be welcome to return. I did not bother testing him to see if he meant it or not.'

Emma made an exasperated sound. 'But don't you see

how you were being as stubborn as him? I am sure he would have welcomed you with open arms if you had come back.'

He gave her a flinty look. 'Still trying to defend him, Emma?' he asked.

She compressed her lips for a moment. 'I'm not doing any such thing; I just think two wrongs never make a right.'

His expression was mocking as he came around to open her door. 'He did a good job on you, didn't he?' he said. 'But then he bought your allegiance.'

Emma stepped out of the car, flinging him a glare over one shoulder. 'Could we talk about something else for a change?' she asked. 'I thought you said this evening's outing was going to be about building our acquaintance, not talking ad infinitum about your late father.'

He shut the car door and took her elbow in the cup of his palm. 'You are right,' he said, and led her towards the restaurant entrance. 'I am not being a very good date so far, am I?'

Emma cast him a glance. 'No, but believe it or not I've had much worse.'

'Is that some sort of compliment?' he asked with the hint of a wry smile.

Emma didn't get the chance to answer as the *maître d'* came to lead them to a table in the little courtyard outside. A short time later they were seated with drinks and a plate of warmed olives and fresh crusty bread set in front of them.

Rafaele picked up his glass and slowly twirled the contents. 'So tell me, Emma,' he said. 'Marriage and kids is high on your to-do list, is that right?'

'If the right person comes along, then yes.'

'Are you one of those young women who have a checklist on what they are looking for in a man?' he asked.

'I don't see a problem with sorting out what you don't want from what you do,' Emma said.

'So what's on your list?'

'The usual things,' she said. 'Faithfulness, a sense of humour and a willingness to be emotionally available.'

'You did not mention money.'

'That's because it's not as important as love.'

He gave her a cynical smile. 'It is always important, Emma,' he said. 'At least it is for all the women I know.'

'I don't agree,' she said. 'Your father is a perfect example of how money doesn't buy love. He had more money than he knew what to do with and yet he didn't have the love and respect of his son.'

'That's because he did not want it,' he said. 'Now, I thought we were not going to talk about him—or have you changed your mind?'

'I'm just trying to understand you, Rafaele.'

'I do not need your understanding, Emma,' he said. 'What is it about women that they always want to pick apart a man's brains? Now, be a good girl and choose something to eat. I am starving after my swim.'

Emma let out a sigh and busied herself with the menu, all the while conscious of the way her body was responding to his close proximity. She knew his desire for her was purely a physical thing on his part; he was between mistresses so why wouldn't he want a quick fling with her to satisfy the primal urge to copulate? Her cheeks grew hot as her brain filled with images of him in the throes of making love, his strong, tanned naked body glistening with sweat as he pumped his essence into the secret heart of her until she…

'Have you had too much sun today, Emma?' Rafaele asked. 'Your cheeks are bright red.'

Emma fanned her face with the menu. 'Um…it's still a bit hot, don't you think?'

'Would you prefer to move indoors where there is air-conditioning?' he asked.

Her eyes fell away from his. 'No…I'm fine out here,' she said and picked up her drink. 'I like being outdoors.'

'I suppose you must spend a great deal of time indoors in the role of a nurse.'

'Yes…if the patient is housebound.'

A small silence passed.

'How ill was my father towards the end?'

Emma brought her eyes back to his. 'He was very ill,' she said softly. 'He had to have high doses of morphine to control the pain so he spent the last couple of weeks drifting in and out of consciousness.'

'So you sat by his side and did everything you could to make him comfortable.'

Emma hunted his expression but found nothing to suggest he was needling her. Instead she thought she saw a flicker of regret pass through his ink-black eyes as they held hers. 'Yes…that is exactly what I did…' She waited a second or two before adding, 'Rafaele…sometimes people change when they know they are about to die. I think your father would have contacted you, but he ran out of strength. I wish now I had done it for him.'

There was a rueful set to his mouth as he spoke. 'I probably would not have listened if you had.' He drew in a breath and added, 'We were too alike if the truth be known. I never quite forgave him for not protecting my mother and he never quite forgave me for not protecting Giovanni.'

'What happened to your brother?' Emma asked.

He picked up his glass and stared down into the contents for a moment. When his eyes came back to hers they had a brittle edge to them that warned her she had come a little too close. 'I did not bring you out this evening to talk about the past and what can never be changed,' he said. 'You have told me all I needed to know and as far as I am concerned I have done the same for you. The rest of my family are dead and buried. I am the only one who remains. Let that be the end of it.'

Emma frowned at him. 'Why do you keep pushing everyone away?' she asked. 'Don't you care how other people feel about you?'

'I am not responsible for other people's feelings,' he said. 'I am only responsible for my own.'

'It sounds to me like you don't have any feelings,' she said. 'Or if you did you switched them off years ago.'

'I have feelings but I choose not to let them get out of control. I do not see the point in being anyone's slave. Once you care too much for someone they can exploit you. That is why I do allow myself to become too attached. It is easier all round. No one gets hurt, or at least not intentionally.'

'So you won't allow yourself to love anyone, not even the women who share your body and your bed,' Emma said in disgust. 'Don't you realise how much you're short-changing yourself?'

He gave her one of his annoyingly indifferent shrugs. 'That is the way it is.'

'Well, I hope that one day you meet someone who turns your neatly controlled world upside down,' she said. 'I hope you fall in love and hard, and then get unceremoniously dumped just so you know what it feels like.'

He gave her an unaffected smile. 'Are you putting a curse on me, Emma?' he asked.

Emma rolled her eyes at him. 'You're impossible. I don't know why I even bother talking to you.'

He smiled lopsidedly as he signalled for the waiter. 'You talk to me because deep down you like me,' he said. 'I am the bad boy you are desperate to reform.'

She gave him a withering look. 'I know when I'm beaten and you are definitely in the too-hard basket,' she said. 'I'm starting to think you're way beyond redemption.'

'Yes, well, that is what my father thought,' he said. 'Didn't he tell you what a wastrel I was?'

Emma frowned at his embittered tone. 'No, he didn't say anything of the sort. I told you, he barely mentioned you the whole time I was living with him. Besides, I didn't want to upset him by prying.'

He smirked. 'It would not do to upset the goose who was about to hand you the golden egg.'

She glared at him heatedly. 'That's just so typical of you,' she said. 'You have a tendency to measure everyone else by your own appalling standards. Just because you regularly use people to get what you want doesn't mean other people will necessarily act that way.'

He held her gaze for several beats. 'I have found most people work things to their advantage,' he said. 'It is hard-wired into human nature.'

'I feel sorry for you,' Emma said. 'You are so cynical you can't possibly enjoy life.'

He gave her an indolent smile. 'On the contrary, Emma I enjoy life very much,' he said. 'I have a good income, good food, good wine and good sex—what more could a man want?'

Emma could feel her face burning, but soldiered on regardless. 'I hope you're not going to conduct any of your sordid little affairs right in front of my nose,' she said. 'It would be totally nauseating to see a host of vacuous women simpering after you like you're some kind of sex god.'

'You surely do not expect me to be celibate for the duration of our marriage, do you?' he asked with a twinkle in his dark gaze.

Emma moistened her dry lips. 'I…no…well…I…'

'I have not been celibate in a very long time,' he said, still watching her with that smouldering gaze.

She shifted restively in her seat. 'Yes, well, the rest will probably do you the world of good, I would have thought.'

'What about you?' he asked.

She looked at him warily. 'W-what about me?'

'What is your longest stint being celibate?'

She dropped her gaze from the penetrating probe of his. 'Um…a fair while…' she answered vaguely.

The waiter came at that moment to take their order, giving Emma a much-needed chance to regroup. She buried her head in the menu, hoping Rafaele couldn't see how ruffled she was at his choice of conversation. She felt so unsophisticated around him, like a child playing at grown-ups. She didn't have the aplomb to laugh off such a personal topic, nor did she have the experience.

Although she knew enough about her body and its responses to know what physical pleasure felt like, somehow she suspected the pleasure Rafaele Fiorenza would dish out would leave her solitary explorations sadly lacking. She had sensed the sensual potency of him that afternoon in the pool. His hardened body brushing against hers had ignited spot fires beneath her skin; she could feel them smouldering even now. Her wayward body was pulsing at the proximity of his long strong legs so close to hers. She had hers tucked as far back beneath her chair as they would go and yet she could still feel the magnetic pull of his body. She couldn't get her mind away from the thought of having his legs entangled with hers the way they had been in the pool, his hair-roughened thighs rubbing against her smoother ones, the heat and power of his erection so tantalisingly close she had felt the throb of his blood pounding against her belly.

The waiter's request for her order brought Emma out of her

reverie and, after choosing the first thing she saw on the menu, she sat back and took a reviving sip of the white wine Rafaele had ordered for her.

He was still watching her in that indolent way of his, as if he was quietly assessing her character. It made her feel a little exposed, as if he could see through the layers of her skull to what she had been thinking about him just moments ago.

'Why are you blushing?' he asked. 'I thought at first it was sunburn but that colour keeps coming and going in your cheeks.'

Emma sat bolt upright. 'I'm not blushing,' she said, even though she knew it wasn't true. She could feel the twin fires burning on her face and wished, not for the first time, she wasn't so out of her depth.

He gave her a knowing smile. 'I think it is rather cute,' he said. 'I do not think I have made a woman blush in years.'

'I'm sure it wasn't from lack of trying,' she quipped wryly.

His smile widened. 'No, that is indeed probably true.'

Emma picked up her glass and took another tentative sip, conscious of his gaze resting on her. Her pulse fluttered in response to his contemplative scrutiny, each of the fine hairs on the back of her neck prickling as if he had touched her there the way he had done earlier in the pool.

'What do you intend to do with your share of the villa at the end of our marriage?' he asked.

She set her glass back down and met his eyes. 'I'm not sure…I haven't thought that far ahead…'

'Would you consider selling it to me?'

She nibbled at her bottom lip for a moment. 'That seems a bit unfair, making you pay for something that really should have been yours in the first place,' she said.

His expression was unreadable. 'You are at perfect liberty to do what you like,' he said. 'We are now joint owners. But if you wish to sell at the end of the time I would like to make the first and final offer.'

'It's a beautiful property,' Emma said. 'It would make a fabulous family home. I wish I could afford to buy you out at the end of the time, but I can't. I would never be able to afford the maintenance costs, for one thing.'

'My half is not going to be for sale,' he said with an implacable edge to his tone.

Emma's forehead wrinkled in a frown. 'It seems rather a large place for a bachelor.'

'Perhaps, but I want to retain ownership regardless.'

'So will you live here permanently?' she asked.

'For some of the year perhaps,' he said. 'I am thinking of appointing a manager to keep the place running while I am away.'

'That sounds like a good idea,' Emma said. 'It would be a shame for it to be empty for long periods.'

He went silent for several moments, his gaze focussed on the contents of his wineglass. 'I have missed the place,' he said almost wistfully. 'I am not quite ready to let it go. There are some ghosts to lay to rest first.'

Emma was starting to see there was more to Rafaele Fiorenza than she had originally thought. It was no wonder he liked to hold the balance of control in all of his relationships. After his experiences as a child he would abhor being vulnerable in any context. He would never allow himself to love anyone in case they turned against him or deserted him.

He reminded her of a wounded wolf who would only attend to his pain in private. She felt her animosity towards him soften, the anger she had felt from the first moment of meeting him melting away to be replaced by compassion and an acute, almost painful desire to understand.

What had put those lines of strain about his mouth or those dark shadows that came and went in the black-brown depths of his gaze? What made his smile teasing and playful one minute and bitter and cynical the next? What would it take to crack open the hard nut of his heart she wondered. What dark secrets were locked away in there?

CHAPTER SIX

AFTER the waiter had brought their meals to the table, Emma concentrated on the delicious seafood risotto set before her, in an attempt to get her emotions in check. What sort of romantic fool would she be to fancy herself in love with Rafaele? She barely knew him and, besides, anyone could see he wasn't a for ever type of guy. She could sense the restlessness in him, the way he worked so hard and played harder, to escape whatever demons drove him.

Emma put her fork down and reached for her wineglass to find his dark, contemplative gaze resting on her. Her heart suddenly felt as if a silk ribbon were being pulled right through the middle of it, making her breath catch in her throat.

'You mentioned the other day you have a sister,' he said. 'What happened to your parents?'

Emma put her glass back down with a little clatter against her dinner plate. 'I would have thought your private investigator contact would have told you when you had him dig up the dirt on my background.'

Rafaele let out a rusty breath. 'I am sorry, Emma, but if you had been in my position you would have done the same.'

She held his gaze for a beat or two, but dropped it to say, 'I haven't seen either of my parents since I was twelve years old when my sister and I were taken into foster care. Our parents were both heroin addicts. The prolonged drug use fried their brains. They died within months of each other, my father from a stab wound from a drug deal gone wrong, my mother from an overdose.'

Rafaele frowned as her quietly spoken words sank in. No wonder she had been so upset about him looking into her background. It also explained why she was so keen to have financial security to make up for what she had missed out on as a child. His own childhood had been painful enough, but to have such incompetent and potentially dangerous parents would have been soul-destroying. He could see now why she had hooked up with his father, to find an older father-figure who would indulge her every whim. Rafaele wouldn't go as far as excusing her for prostituting herself in such a way, but at least he understood her motive for doing so.

'I am sorry you had such a rough time of it,' he said. 'I have always thought it is a pity one cannot choose one's own parents. It would certainly make life easier for many children growing up.'

Her eyes came back to his. 'I guess so…but it's a parent's responsibility to be the adult in the relationship once children come along. Children don't ask to be born. They deserve to be loved no matter what.'

'That is one of the reasons I do not want to have children,' he said. 'It is too risky. How can I guarantee I will even like the child, let alone love it?'

Emma felt an inexplicable pang deep inside at his words. 'I'm sure you would love your own flesh and blood,' she said. 'One of the few benefits of coming from a difficult background is recognising the pitfalls to avoid when you become a parent yourself. You wouldn't make the same mistakes your father made, I'm sure of it.'

His smile was a little crooked. 'No, but I would probably make new ones,' he said. 'Then in thirty-odd years I would have a son or daughter who hated my guts. No way am I going to put my head in that particular noose. I am staying out of the parent trap.'

'But what if it were to happen?' Emma asked, still frowning slightly. 'What if one of your mistresses got pregnant by accident?'

The line of his mouth tightened a fraction. 'Firstly I would find it a little hard to believe it was an accident,' he said. 'I always take precautions and so do my sexual partners. In fact I insist on it.'

'Precautions can fail,' she pointed out. 'My sister Simone fell pregnant while on the pill. She was only nineteen at the time. If that happened to one of your partners would you expect her to have a termination?'

'I realise that is a decision best left to the woman concerned,' he said. 'An unwanted pregnancy is devastating to many women. I would not insist on her going through with it unless she was convinced it was the only option for her.'

'Wouldn't you want to be involved in its upbringing?' Emma asked.

He drew in a breath and reached for his glass once more. 'I am not sure a child should be in regular contact with a reluctant father. Children are not stupid. They work out pretty quickly who is genuine and who is not.'

Emma frowned at him. 'But don't all children deserve to have contact with both of their parents if at all possible?' she asked.

'In an ideal world, yes,' he said. 'But it is hard for men these days. It seems to me we are damned if we do and damned if we do not. We are called selfish for not wanting to procreate, and then if we do agree to father a child we are the worst in the world for not contributing enough in terms of housework or child care, even though we might be working every hour God sends to keep food on the table.'

'I hadn't really thought about it from that angle,' she confessed. 'But I still want to have a family. I just have to find a man who wants the same thing.'

'You have got plenty of time yet,' Rafaele said. 'Why not have a bit of fun while you still can?'

She gave him a guarded glance. 'I hope you're not suggesting what I think you're suggesting.'

He reached across the table and picked up her left hand, the pad of his thumb stroking over the backs of her fingers. 'What about it, Emma?' he asked. 'Want to have some fun with me before we call it quits?'

'I'm not sure it would be all that much fun for me,' she said with a haughty little glare.

He brought her hand to his mouth, the slight rasp of his skin against her fingers making her stomach fold over. 'I would make sure it was fun for you, *poco moglie di miniera*,' he said, and translated in a low sexy drawl, 'little wife of mine.'

She tried to pull out of his hold, but his fingers around hers subtly tightened. 'You're only doing this because you see me as a novelty. It's because I won't fall at your feet just like every other poor deluded woman out there, isn't it?'

The movement of his lips as he gave her a wry smile grazed her bent knuckles, sending another ripple of awareness through her body from her breasts to her thighs. 'I admit you are becoming a bit of a challenge to me,' he said. 'I have not had to work so hard at getting a woman to agree to have an affair with me before.'

Emma gave him another glare as she pulled her hand out of his, this time with success. 'I thought you said you weren't interested in sleeping with someone your father had slaked his lust on first? Those were your exact words, weren't they?'

His eyes held hers fast. 'Did you sleep with him, Emma?'

She returned his level stare. 'No, I did not.'

Rafaele sat back in his chair and surveyed her heightened colour, wondering if she was lying to him or not. He wanted to believe her, but knowing his father as he did he couldn't imagine him handing over half of his estate without some sort of inducement from her. His father had always been so mean with money; it didn't seem possible he would have given something away for free.

Admittedly Emma was nothing like any of his father's previous mistresses, but that didn't mean he hadn't fallen for her understated beauty and beguiling aura of innocence. Rafaele could see beyond the prim and proper façade she adopted to the passionate woman simmering beneath. She was a feisty little thing with her flashing grey-blue eyes and pouting mouth, her sensual allure so powerful he could barely keep his hands off her every time she was in the same room as him.

He wondered if she was holding him at bay deliberately. Had she done that with his father, leading him on and on until he finally agreed to give her what she wanted? If so, what was it she wanted from him? She already had half of the estate secure in her hands. Nothing he could do or say could take it away from her. But did she want more, and, if so, what?

'If you say you did not sleep with him, then I suppose I shall have to accept that,' he said after a pause.

'I have no reason to lie to you about something like that,' she said. 'What could I hope to gain by doing so?'

'I am not sure,' he said, rubbing at his jaw. 'I am still trying to figure that part out. Eighteen months ago you had not even met my father, now you own half of his estate. I am trying to join the dots but so far with little success.'

Emma reached for her glass. 'Maybe he wanted you to

learn to trust people,' she said. 'Perhaps he sensed I wouldn't do the wrong thing by you.'

'Interesting theory, Emma,' he said with an unreadable smile. 'But I wonder if he really knew you. You caught him at a vulnerable time. He was dying and his judgement may well have been impaired. For all I know you could have talked him into this madcap scheme.'

Emma compressed her lips. 'Of course *you* would think that, wouldn't you?' she said. 'You don't want me to be anything but a scam artist, do you? What if you're wrong about me, Rafaele? What then?'

He studied her for a lengthy moment. 'If that is the case I guess I will have to get down on bended knee and beg your forgiveness,' he said. 'But it is hardly something you would be able to prove either way, is it?'

Emma could think of a very good way of proving it, but didn't like to inform him of it. It wasn't that she was ashamed of her inexperience; it was more a case of not wanting him to ridicule her. Somehow that seemed particularly important. Besides, she could just imagine what he would say. She could even imagine his teasing smile.

'I don't have to prove anything to you,' she said instead. 'You can believe me or not, it makes no difference to the truth.'

'So you don't do recreational, just-for-the-hang-of-it sex?'

'No.'

'Pity,' he said. 'I think we could be dynamite together. Fire meets ice, that sort of thing.'

'I think any woman with half a brain would give you a wide berth,' she said. 'You won't commit, you're incapable of falling in love and you don't want kids. For the thinking woman you're a very bad deal, Rafaele.'

He gave her a bone-melting smile. 'But I make up for it in other ways. Even thinking women like hot sex, do they not?'

Emma hated that she blushed so readily. 'I can't speak for other women, but personally I would rather share my body with a man who treats me as an equal, not as a sex object.'

'I do not see you as a sex object, Emma. I just think we could be really good together.'

'Oh, yes, but for how long?'

He gave a could-mean-anything shrug. 'I am not one for setting time limits,' he said. 'Physical attraction has its own timetable.'

'Yes, but in your case it lasts about as long as the life cycle of a flea,' she said. 'Or maybe even a gnat.'

He gave a low chuckle of laughter. 'You are *so* damned cute. I bet you do not even know how long a gnat's life cycle is.'

Emma tried to purse her lips, but somehow it ended in a lopsided smile. 'You're incorrigible. You really are.'

He picked up her hand again and brushed his lips over the back of her knuckles, his dark-as-midnight gaze holding hers. 'But you like me anyway, right, *mio piccolo*?'

Emma didn't answer but the words seemed to ring in the silence all the same: *I like you. I like you too much.*

CHAPTER SEVEN

THE drive back to The Villa Fiorenza took only a few minutes but Emma suddenly found she didn't want the evening to be over. Rafaele had relaxed over dessert and coffee, chatting to her about his work as a share trader, telling her some amusing anecdotes about some of the people he'd met and the places he'd visited. She knew she was being a fool for letting her guard down around him, but for some reason the cold breath of common sense couldn't seem to penetrate the warm mantle of complacency that had settled around her in his company.

As he led the way to the front door of the grand old house, Emma could smell the pungent clove-like scent of night stocks from the massive herbaceous border running along one side of the property. The purple and white pendulous blooms of sweetly scented wisteria hung in a fragrant array from the trellis on one of the walls, and the melodious twinkle of the wind chimes hanging in the summer house carried over the garden on the slight breeze, setting an atmosphere that was as intoxicating as a mind-altering drug.

'Why don't we take a nightcap out to the arbour?' Rafaele said once they were inside. 'It is too nice a night to be indoors.'

'That sounds lovely,' Emma said, wondering if he had somehow read her mind. She had been thinking how nice it would be to sit out in the garden, breathing in the fragrant air and looking up at the peepholes of stars and planets in the dark blue blanket of the sky.

A few minutes later she followed him out to the summer house, minus her heels, the soft, slightly damp carpet of the springy lawn tickling the soles of her bare feet.

Rafaele handed her a cognac and patted the swing seat beside him. 'You look like a nymph or a sprite,' he said with a smile.

Emma returned his smile with a warm one of her own. 'I love nights like this,' she said, curling her toes as she sat on the seat next to him. 'I love the sounds and smells of a garden late at night. It's like another world out here.'

He placed his foot against the frame of the arched doorway to set the swing in motion. The gentle rocking motion brought their bodies closer together on the seat. Emma could feel the strong length of his thigh within a breath of her own, her shoulder brushing against his upper arm. Her skin tingled as he laid his left arm over the back of the seat, his fingers within touching distance of the nape of her neck. It would be so easy to turn and face him, to reach up and stroke her fingers over the lean planes and angles of his face, to explore the contours of his sensual mouth.

'You have not touched your cognac,' he said, looking at the glass she was cradling in her hands.

'I haven't got much of a head for alcohol,' Emma confessed. 'The wine we had at dinner has already addled my brain.' *And my common sense*, she thought wryly as she placed her untouched glass on the nearest ledge.

The long silence was measured by the sound of crickets chirruping in the background, the soft plop of a frog landing in the lily pond sounding like a distant gunshot.

Rafaele turned to look at her. 'Did you ever bring my father out here?' he asked.

Emma couldn't read his expression, his face was in shadow, but she sensed tension in the question. 'Yes…a couple of times,' she answered. 'He found it peaceful and the fresh air was good for him after being confined indoors for so long.'

Another silence slipped past.

In spite of the darkness Emma could feel the slow burn of his gaze as it held hers. 'What are you thinking about, Emma?' he asked.

She self-consciously tucked a loose strand of hair behind her ear. 'I was thinking how we're probably going to be eaten alive by mosquitoes,' she said with a rueful tilt of her mouth.

The white slash of his smile cut across his shadowed face. 'Or what about gnats?'

She screwed up her mouth at him. 'Do gnats bite?'

'I am not sure,' he said as he set his glass to one side before turning back to face her.

Emma sat very still as he lifted his hand to her face, his index finger tracing over the curve of her top lip. She couldn't breathe; she couldn't even speak, so mesmerising was his feather-light touch. She watched as in slow motion his head came down, his mouth so close she could feel the warmth of his breath skating over her lips. She sucked in a sharp little breath as his lips pressed against hers, once, twice, and then the third time with increasing pressure.

His mouth was like a brand, searing her lips with the imprint of his, stirring her senses into a frenzy of heady excitement. The first slow and yet determined stroke of his tongue against the seam of her lips sent her pulse skyrocketing, the rasp of his masculine jaw with its stubbly growth against the tender skin of her face making her feel utterly feminine in a way she had never felt before.

He explored every corner of her mouth in a leisurely fashion, the drugging movements of his mouth on hers making her forget all about her reasons for not getting involved with him. Desire began to pulse hot and strong in her veins with each thrust of his tongue against hers, the erotic promise in his kiss unmistakable.

His teeth nibbled at the fullness of her bottom lip in tiny, tantalising tug-and-release bites that made her legs turn to water. Her feminine core melted, she could feel the dew of desire anointing her intimately, her breasts swollen and aching for the attention of his hands and lips and tongue.

He pulled her to her feet, her legs hardly able to keep her upright as his mouth lifted off hers to blaze a fiery trail of kisses along the sensitive skin of her neck, each hot blast of his breath inciting her need of him to fever pitch. She was melting in his arms, discovering a passionate facet to her personality she would never have believed had existed until now. Where was her self-control? Where was her level-headedness and cool composure? They seemed to have been swept up in the conflagration of her senses under the sensual mastery of his touch.

His lower body ground against hers, leaving her in no doubt of his arousal. It was thick and hard against her, making her body tremble all over with a clawing need for fulfilment.

His mouth came back to hers with renewed fervour, the pressure of his kiss increasing as his erection burned with insistent force against her traitorous flesh. She could feel the hollow ache of her body, the tight walls of her womanhood preparing for the onslaught of his thickened presence. She felt as if she would die if he didn't bring to completion what he had started. Her body was crying out for release from this sensual torment. There was no part of her that wasn't sizzling from the heat of his touch. He was like a fire in her blood; somehow he had circumvented her firewall of common sense and turned her into a desperate wanton, a slave to the passion he had awakened.

Rafaele lifted his mouth off hers to look down at her with eyes dark with desire. 'Let's take this inside—or shall we get it over with right here on the floor?'

Emma flinched as her conscience gave her an unwelcome but timely nudge. No wonder he thought she was his for the asking. She had practically melted in his arms. Shame flooded her cheeks and to disguise it she stepped out of his hold, her expression full of cold disdain. 'You might not have liked him much, but at least your father had much more class than you,' she said with a cutting edge to her tone. 'He would never have dreamed of insulting me the way you have done.'

His eyes became diamond hard. 'What is wrong, Emma? Are you expecting a little more finesse? I thought you would be used to doing it rough since you have been servicing my father. He would not have been too fussy about where he had you. Or maybe he got sentimental in his old age and whispered sweet nothings in your ear.'

'That's a disgusting thing to say!' Emma said, her face fire-engine red.

'What about it, Emma?' he said. 'How about we get down and dirty while we are married? You are up for it, I can tell.'

She gave him a paint-stripping glare. 'I wouldn't dream of tainting myself with the likes of you.'

His smile was deliberately taunting. 'I can afford you, Emma. If it is more money you want I have plenty of it. I have ten times the wealth of my father.'

'I want nothing from you,' she bit out. 'I would rather die.'

'You are such a transparent liar,' he said. 'If the way you kissed me is anything to go by I can almost guarantee it will not be long before we end up sharing much more than this villa.'

'I did *not* kiss you,' Emma said through tight lips. 'You kissed me. You took me completely by surprise.'

His eyes began to glint. 'Ditto. You totally rocked me.

had no idea how passionate you are behind that school-marmish façade you are so fond of displaying to the world. But it is all an act, isn't it, Emma? That is how you got my father's attention, wasn't it? You reeled him in like a minnow on a line.'

Emma felt like slapping him, but in truth she was frustrated at herself for falling under his sensual spell so incautiously. How could she have been so stupid? He had wined and dined her, setting the scene for seduction, and she had fallen for it so readily. It made her feel so foolish but also very hurt.

Deeply hurt.

He had no feelings for her. He despised her. How could she have been lulled into thinking anything else? Tears suddenly blurred her vision and desperate to keep them hidden, she pushed past him with a hastily muttered goodnight.

'Emma?' He caught up to her in a couple of strides and tipped her face to one of the fingers of light coming from the villa. He frowned as he dabbed at a rolling tear with the blunt pad of his finger. 'Tears?' he asked, sounding surprised.

Emma shoved his hand away and glared at him. 'You must think I'm so naïve,' she bit out. 'You think you can just crook your finger and have me dive head first into your bed, don't you?'

'It was just a kiss, Emma,' he said in a dry tone.

'It was *not* just a kiss!' she railed at him.

'What was it then?'

'It was a blatant attempt to seduce me, that's what it was,' she said with a livid grey-blue glare.

'If I was serious about seducing you, Emma, you would be flat on your back by now and letting the neighbours know in no uncertain terms how much you were enjoying it,' he said with a smug little smile.

Emma opened and closed her mouth at his audacity. 'I can't believe you just said that!'

'I said it because it is true,' he said. 'I am not going to play games with you, *cara*. I am prepared to bed you any time you like. But that is all I am offering, so you had better be clear on that. No strings, just good old-fashioned bed-wrecking sex. Take it or leave it.'

She threw him a caustic look. 'I'll leave it, thank you.'

'Fine, but if you change your mind just let me know,' he said. 'I think we could be dynamite together.'

'I won't be changing my mind,' Emma said, with perhaps not as much conviction as she would have liked. His evocative comments had unravelled her resolve to an alarming degree. Her body was on fire just thinking about the pleasure he was promising. She was in no doubt of his ability to be as good as his word. She could see the smouldering look in his dark eyes. She could still feel the imprint of his lips on hers. Her mouth was tingling even now, the tiny nerves beneath her skin leaping and jumping from the passionate pressure of his. What was it about this man that made her feel so out of control? Was it because she had decided he was off limits? Was some perverse part of her determined to have him in spite of her convictions?

He had made it more than clear what he wanted. He was attracted to her certainly, but only as a means to an end. Once he got what he wanted she would be discarded, just as he had discarded his numerous other mistresses.

It hurt Emma to realise how much she wanted it to be different. How had that happened in such a short space of time? She had hated him the first time she had met him and yet it was difficult to dredge up such intense feelings now. There was something about him that drew her in like a moth to a deadly flame. He intrigued her, he excited her and he made her feel things she had never felt before. She truly wondered if she would ever be the same now she had tasted his potent passion on her lips. Would every kiss she received from this point on be measured by the heat and fire of his? Would any future lover of hers fall short of his blistering benchmark? Would she always feel short-changed and frustrated as a result?

'I'm going inside,' she said, turning away again.

His hand stalled her. 'Wait.'

Emma felt the steel bracelet of his fingers and suppressed a tiny shiver. She looked up at his face, her breath catching at the back of her throat at the intensity of his dark gaze as it meshed with hers. 'I-I can't do this, Rafaele…' she said. 'It's not right.'

His thumb found her pulse, the drumbeat of her heart beating against his skin. 'But you want to, don't you, Emma?' he asked softly.

Emma compressed her lips to stop them from trembling, her heart pumping so hard she could feel it against her sternum. It would be so easy to throw caution to one side and step into his arms. It would be so easy to press her still-swollen lips to the sculptured curve of his.

It would be all too easy to fall in love with him…

'Go on, admit it,' he said. 'You want me just as much as I want you.'

She drew in a prickly breath. 'I want a lot of things I can't have, Rafaele,' she said. 'Wanting something doesn't make it right.'

The hard look came back into his eyes. 'Is it because of my father?' he asked. 'Do you still have feelings for him even though he is dead?'

Emma frowned at him. 'Why must you persist with this?' she asked. 'Just let it go, for God's sake.'

'Damn it, Emma,' he growled. 'I hate the thought of you with him. It sickens me to my stomach. I cannot get it out of my mind. I keep seeing him pawing at you like some animal.'

She gave him an ironic look. 'Isn't that what you've been doing to me?'

His brows snapped together and his hand fell away from her wrist. 'Is that what you think?' he asked.

Emma wished she hadn't said it. The anger was coming off him in waves. The air crackled with it, the tension building to an intolerable level. 'No…no, of course not,' she said. 'I'm sorry…I shouldn't have said that.'

'No, you should not,' he said through tight lips. 'You were with me all the way, Emma. You were hot for it.'

She felt her face fire with colour at his blunt crudity and her own traitorous transparency. 'You know, I was really starting to like you earlier this evening, but now I think I will stick to my first impression of you,' she said with a blistering glare.

He gave her a mocking smile, but anger was still glittering in his eyes. 'And what might that be?'

She pulled in a tight little breath. 'You're an unscrupulous, selfish bastard who uses people without conscience.'

'And do you know what my impression of you is, Emma?' he threw back.

'That's hardly necessary considering you've used every available opportunity to tell me,' she said with bitterness sharpening her tone. 'A tart, a whore, a slut, the list goes on and on.'

'You are a clever little cat with an eye on the main chance,' he said as if she hadn't spoken. 'You want it all, don't you, Emma? That's what you are counting on, isn't it? That I will walk away before the year is up and by doing so hand you the lot.'

'I don't want you to walk away from what is rightly yours,' she said. 'I'm trying my best to do the right thing by you. I admit there are certain advantages for me, but I'm not interested in taking your inheritance from you.'

'But you want the money.'

'Yes, but not for the reasons you think,' she said.

Rafaele looked into her grey-blue eyes and wondered if she was being straight with him. He wasn't used to trusting people, but he found he wanted to trust her. She was getting under his skin in a way he had never believed possible.

He hadn't thought a kiss could reveal so much. He had kissed a lot of women in his time, but no one had affected him quite as Emma did. The shy hesitancy of her responses had been totally enthralling. He could still taste her sweetness in his mouth. He could still feel the soft press of her slim body against his; it had left a branding outline on his flesh.

His desire for her was even now pulsing through his blood. He could feel it charging through his veins, making him hard at the thought of sinking into her velvet warmth. He had never wanted a woman more than this one. She awakened every primal desire in his body. Her sensual allure was totally bewitching, which was no doubt why his father had fallen under her spell.

But he wasn't a fool like his father. He would have her on his terms and his terms only, even if it took him every bit of the next twelve months to achieve it.

'What do you want the money for?' he asked.

'It's for my sister, Simone.'

He frowned. 'Your sister?'

She nodded. 'She lost her husband when my niece was a baby. She has never dated anyone else until recently, but it turned out to be a total disaster. He left her with massive debts. He fraudulently used her name for a loan with a dodgy creditor who was making some nasty threats about repaying it.' She gave a jagged little sigh and continued, 'I sent the money I got when I married you to her.'

Rafaele kept his eyes on her. 'It all seems rather convenient, does it not?' he said. 'It seems to me that my father's death came at rather a good time for you and your sister.'

Her grey-blue eyes flared with shock or was it anger? He couldn't quite make up his mind. 'Are you suggesting I did something to hurry up your father's death?' she asked.

'You stood to gain by it, though, did you not?'

Her face paled. 'I told you, I had no idea what was in your father's will. This is your home, Rafaele. I think deep down your father wanted you to have it.'

'He went a strange way about it,' Rafaele growled.

'Yes, but sometimes the things we have to work the hardest for are the things we end up valuing the most,' she said. 'Perhaps your father was trying to tell you something.'

'My father was always trying to tell me something,' he said bitterly. 'Like how I was the one who should have died that day, not Giovanni.'

Emma stared at him with wide, shocked eyes. 'Surely he didn't say that?'

He gave her a grim look. 'He did not need to. It is true. I should have been the one to die.'

She put a hand to her chest. 'Oh, Rafaele…'

'I was the older brother, I was supposed to protect him, but instead I killed him.'

Emma felt her stomach give a sudden lurch. The atmosphere between them had changed. She hesitantly pressed him for more details. 'W-what happened?'

His eyes looked soulless and bleak. 'I was teaching Giovanni to play cricket… It was his turn to bat. I didn't think I had thrown the ball too hard, I was always so careful, but somehow it hit him on the temple and he fell like a stone.'

Emma gasped. 'No one could blame you for that. *No one*,' she insisted hoarsely.

'Perhaps some would say I was just a child myself and could not be held responsible,' he said. 'But I did not see it that way and neither did my father. I spent the next eight years apologising for my existence. Every time my father looked at me I saw the hatred and disappointment on his face.'

Emma felt her heart tighten at what he had gone through.

She could see the pain etched on his face, the deep grooves at the side of his mouth and the almost permanent lines on his forehead making her realise he was not the shallow, selfish man she had first thought. He was a deep and complex man, a man who had been cruelly hurt by the vicissitudes of life, a man who had locked away his heart to avoid further pain. A man almost crushed with a guilt that should never have been laid upon his shoulders.

A man she was one step closer to falling in love with…

'Thank you for telling me about it,' she said softly. 'I can only imagine how painful it must be to do so. It explains a lot…about everything…'

'This place is full of my guilt, Emma,' he said, waving his hand towards the giant shadow of the house to the left of him. 'Even the floorboards creak with it. My father left Giovanni's room the way it was to drive home the point.'

Emma bit her lip. 'Maybe you're reading too much into that,' she said. 'A lot of parents find it very hard to let go after the death of a child. Getting rid of their things is like saying they didn't exist. It's a way of holding on to them for as long as possible.'

'For twenty-three bloody years?' he asked.

She let out a little sigh. 'I guess everyone has their own time frame.'

'Stop defending him, Emma,' he ground out. 'He wanted me to suffer.'

'You were ten years old, Rafaele. Just a little boy. You were not to blame. It was an accident. Can't you see that?'

'Do you know what it is like, Emma?' he asked, his dark gaze almost black with pain. 'Do you know what it's like to be holding your dead brother's body in your arms, begging God or whoever is out there to breathe life back into his lungs until your throat is red raw from screaming?'

Emma felt a sob catch at the back of her throat. 'I–I'm so sorry…'

He raked a hand through his hair. 'I would have given anything to save him. We had already been through so much with the loss of our mother. He looked to me for everything, but in the end I killed him.'

Emma couldn't speak. The anguish on his face was too heart-wrenching. She wanted to reach out and hold him to her, to offer what comfort she could, to help him move on from the pain of the past.

'After we came home from Giovanni's funeral my father didn't speak to me for months afterwards. He could barely be in the same room as me. I was packed off to boarding school and on the rare occasions when my father was here at the villa when I was on holiday he kept himself busy with his latest mistress, usually a young woman not much older than me. After I finished school I left the country. I had no reason to think he was anything but relieved when I finally packed my bags and left.'

Emma put a hand on his arm. 'Rafaele…you need to forgive yourself,' she said. 'You can't carry that guilt for ever. Your father was wrong to put that on you, but perhaps he was feeling guilty himself. Why wasn't he out there playing cricket with his young sons? Have you ever thought of that?'

'I have thought about it a lot,' he said. 'But even if he did feel marginally responsible he never let on. I do not even know where he was the day Giovanni died. He would never say. All I know is it seemed an eternity before he got back…'

Emma brushed her tears away with the back of her hand. 'I'm so sorry…so very sorry…'

He drew in a deep uneven breath as he looked at the house. 'I am going to make a start on clearing out Giovanni's room in the next day or so. It should have been done years ago.'

'Would you like me to help you?' she asked.

He turned back to look at her again. 'No, thank you all the same. This is one job I probably need to do alone.'

A little silence crept from the shadows of the garden towards them.

Rafaele got to his feet. 'I am going to take a walk around the gardens,' he said. 'Do not wait up. I will see you in the morning.'

She stepped up on tiptoe and pressed a soft-as-air kiss to his cheek. 'Goodnight, Rafaele,' she whispered.

Rafaele stood and watched as she made her way back to the house, the soft, ghost-like tread of her bare feet making no sound on the dew-kissed, spongy grass.

CHAPTER EIGHT

WHEN Emma came downstairs the next morning Rafaele was out on the sun-drenched terrace with a pot of freshly brewed coffee beside him, the morning paper spread out before him on the wrought-iron garden setting. He was dressed similarly to her, in a close fitting white T-shirt and shorts to counteract the early heat of the day. He had recently showered, his hair was still damp and she could smell the sharp citrus tang of his aftershave as she came closer.

He turned his head as he heard her approach, his expression giving no hint of the anguish she had seen there the night before. 'There is enough for two if you would like some,' he said, indicating the coffee-pot with a careless waft of his hand.

'Thanks,' she said. 'I never feel truly awake until I've had my first caffeine hit.'

'I will go and get a cup for you,' he said, rising to his feet. 'Would you like a croissant? I jogged down to the bakery first thing this morning.'

Emma gave him a rueful smile. 'You're making me feel guilty, talking about early-morning jogs,' she said. 'I'm not normally so lazy, but I didn't sleep well last night.'

His expression was mask-like, although Emma thought

she saw something flicker in his eyes as they held hers. 'I hope it wasn't something I said.'

She let out a tiny sigh. 'It was everything you said. I feel like I've totally misjudged you. You're not the person I thought you were. I'm sorry. I hope you can find it in yourself to forgive me.' She looked up at him appealingly and added softly, 'I'd like us…I'd like us to be friends.'

The silence stretched for a moment or two.

'Is that pity I hear in your voice, Emma?' he asked in a flint-like tone.

She frowned at him. 'No…no, of course not,' she said. 'I'm just glad I now know what happened to your brother and how it affected you and your father's relationship. Life has been very hard on you. I didn't realise how hard until last night.'

His eyes glittered darkly as they seared hers. 'So it explains why I am a complete and utter bastard, does it, Emma?'

She compressed her lips. 'That's a choice you make,' she said. 'You don't have to be that way. Lots of people have tragic backgrounds and yet manage to move on without letting it ruin their life and all their relationships.'

'I have not let it ruin my life,' he said. 'And as for my relationships, that is my business and my business alone.'

'I think you have let it ruin your life,' Emma countered. 'You lock yourself away from feeling. I suspect you've done it for years. You're doing it now. As soon as anyone gets close you put up a wall of resistance. You let your guard down with me last night and now you're regretting it. That's why you're being so cutting and unfriendly towards me now.'

He gave a mocking laugh. 'So little Emma now wants to be friends with me, does she?'

She tightened her mouth without answering.

He stepped closer and, capturing her chin between his finger and thumb, tipped her gaze to meet his. 'How far are you prepared to take this offer of friendship?' he asked. 'All the way upstairs to my bed?'

Emma felt her stomach go hollow as he brought his hard male body even closer. Her tongue darted out to moisten her lips, her heart beginning to ram against her ribcage as she felt his arrant maleness springing to turgid life against her. He placed a hand in the small of her back, pressing her even closer so she felt the pounding of his blood against her softness.

And then his head came down…

The kiss was explosive. Their tongues wrestled and tangled, darted and dived and submitted and conquered simultaneously. Emma became breathless with growing excitement, her body on fire as his mouth commandeered hers with bruising passion. Her lips throbbed with the pressure, she even thought she could taste blood at one point, but wasn't sure if it was hers or his, as she had nipped at his bottom lip with just as much fervour as he had hers.

His mouth was still locked on hers as he shoved aside the thin straps of her top and bra, his hands cupping the slight weight of her breasts, her pert nipples driving into the moist heat of his palm. The tingling pleasure wasn't nearly enough. Emma wanted more of his touch and leaned into him, whimpering her need into the hot cavern of his mouth.

Her breathing came to a screeching halt as he lifted his mouth off hers to suckle on each breast in turn. She arched her back as the rasp of his tongue laved her tender flesh, her fingers grasping him by the shoulders to anchor herself as sensation after sensation coursed through her.

He brought his mouth back to hers, his tongue a thrusting force she welcomed with the shy dart of her own. She heard him make a sound at the back of his throat and her skin lifted in goose-bumps of feverish excitement at how she was affecting him. She could feel the heat and weight of his arousal pressing against her and reached boldly between their locked bodies to explore it with her fingers. He groaned again as she brushed her fingertips over the summer-weight linen of his shorts, the proud bulge of his body making her feel heady with feminine power. She wanted to touch him intimately, she wanted to feel the satin of his flesh in her hands, to shape him, to feel the surge of his blood, to tantalise him the way he was tantalising her.

'God, I want you,' he said against her mouth. 'I am going crazy with you touching me like that.'

His feverish confession incited Emma to slide down the zipper on his shorts, her searching fingers moving aside the final barrier of his underwear. Her breath caught as she felt his body leap against her hand, the smoothness and strength of him rising out of the springy masculine hair making her belly crawl with desire. She looked down at him, her eyes going wide at the size of him as he quivered against her tentative feather-light touch.

'Harder, Emma,' he said on a gasping breath. 'Touch me harder and faster.'

She did as he said, her own body quaking with the need to feel him fill her and explode with the banked-up energy she could feel throbbing against the pads of her fingertips.

He placed his hand over hers, stilling the movement. 'Stop,' he said, giving a little shudder. 'I am going to come right here and now if you do not stop.'

'Would that be a problem?' Emma asked on an impulse too strong to withstand. The desire to pleasure him was suddenly irresistible. She wanted to see how much he wanted her, to witness the way his body responded to her caressing touch.

His eyes were so dark she couldn't see his pupils. 'I am in the habit of abiding by the principle ladies come first,' he said.

Emma quickly made a token effort to locate her reasons

for not sleeping with him, but not one of them was at the forefront of her brain. All she could think of was the thousands of reasons she wanted to be in his arms: the passion, the excitement, the pleasure and the thrill of experiencing the rapture of his possession.

But if her mind was her traitor, so too was her body. It was already pressing against him insistently as his mouth came down to hers, her arms going around his neck, not even a sound of resistance escaping from her throat as he lifted her bodily in his arms and carried her into the house.

He didn't take her as far as his bedroom. The largest sitting room was the closest, and, letting her slowly slide down the length of his aroused body to stand on the carpeted floor in front of him, he looked down at her with that scorching gaze of his.

'Take your clothes off,' he commanded.

That should have been Emma's cue to stop this madness, but somehow her hands went to the bottom of her top and pulled it over her head, dropping it to the floor at her feet. She hesitated for the briefest moment before taking off her shorts, leaving her standing before him in her pink lace bra and knickers.

'And the rest,' he said, his dark eyes feasting on her hungrily.

Emma felt her belly give two hard kicks of desire. 'You first,' she said with a little hitch of her chin.

His lips twitched slightly, but then he wrenched his T-shirt over his head before stepping out of his shorts and underwear, his legs apart, his arms folded across his broad chest.

Emma swallowed as she looked at him. He looked magnificent, lean and tanned and toned and devastatingly virile. His erection was bobbing slightly, as if eager to get on with business. She couldn't take her eyes off it. Had *she* done that to him?

'Come here,' he said with a glittering look.

She took one shaky step towards him. 'Rafaele…I—'

He placed the end of his fingertip against her lips. 'You talk too much,' he said. 'Right now I want you to feel.'

Emma was awash with feeling; her entire body was tingling and leaping with excitement at what was ahead. She felt as if she had waited her whole life for this moment. He was her nemesis—the one man who had tempted her out of her sensual stasis.

It was a shock to her how much she wanted him. It pulsed through her with such force it almost frightened her. She had been so very determined not to succumb to his potent sexual allure and yet here she was quivering to feel him thrust inside her.

She put her hands behind her back to unhook her bra, her breathing ragged as he watched her reveal her nakedness. His eyes darkened and his throat moved up and down as she tugged her lacy knickers down. She saw his eyes flare as he took in her feminine form, a pulse leaping in his jaw as he fought for control.

'You are beautiful,' he said huskily.

Emma felt her heart swell at the compliment. She had never considered herself anything other than average, and yet somehow now in front of him she felt as if she were the most exquisite creature on earth. Her natural shyness fell away, her desire to pleasure him knowing no bounds as she stepped up against him, her softness against his hardness. 'So are you,' she said in a breathless whisper as her hands skated over his chest before going lower.

He sucked in a breath as her fingers trailed through the dark hair that arrowed downwards, his erection thick and hard against the enclosure of her hand. Such power and yet such vulnerability, Emma thought as she stroked him.

'Enough,' he groaned and pushed her hand away. 'I want to taste you.'

Emma shivered as he pushed her down to the floor, the almost primitive urgency thrilling her. He parted her thighs, his warm breath like a caress as he kissed his way up from her knees to the secret heart of her. She drew in a rasping breath as his fingers tenderly parted her feminine folds, the first stroke of his tongue making her back arch off the floor. A flood of sensations swamped her, tingling electric-like feelings that left her mindless as her body's impulses took over. She felt the first flicker of a spasm and shrank back from it in nervous apprehension.

Rafaele's hands on her thighs softened into a soothing caress. 'Relax for me, Emma,' he said. 'Go with it, *cara.*'

'I-I can't…' she said breathlessly.

'Yes, you can,' he said gently. 'I am probably rushing you. I will slow down.'

It's not that, Emma wanted to say, but somehow couldn't quite bring herself to do so. How could she tell him she was a virgin? After what he had assumed had occurred between her and his father would he even believe her?

As if he sensed her uneasiness with such raw intimacy he moved up her body, kissing her deeply as his weight pinned her beneath him. She sighed with pleasure as his erection nudged against her moist folds, the sensation of him being so close but not close enough almost unbearable. She began to squirm under him, her body instinctively searching for his.

Suddenly he was there, in one slick, tearing thrust he was inside her, the gasping cry of discomfort she tried to suppress not quite as inaudible as she had hoped it would be.

He reared back, his weight resting on his arms as he looked down at her. 'I am rushing you, aren't I?' he said. 'I thought you were ready for me. You felt ready for me. I am sorry— did I hurt you?'

She shook her head, her bottom lip caught between her teeth.

His eyes narrowed slightly. 'What's going on?' he asked.

Emma felt tears prick at the backs of her eyes. 'I should have told you...I'm sorry...'

His gaze narrowed even further. 'Told me what?'

She took a gulping swallow. 'I've never done this before... you know...had sex...'

Rafaele stared at her in stupefaction. *'What?'*

She bit her lip again, her eyes sprouting tears. 'I know I should have told you but I didn't think you'd believe me...'

He felt a knife twist in his chest. 'You mean you're...you're a...a *virgin*?'

She winced as if he had just insulted her. 'Do you have to say it like that?' she asked. 'It's not something I should be ashamed of.'

He stared at her for a moment, his mind whirling. What had he done? Oh, dear God, what had he done? He thought of all the times he had thrown his filthy accusations at her, never for a moment thinking she had been anything other than the conniving slut he'd believed her to be.

His father hadn't slept with her.

It was almost too much for him to take in. Why had his father left things the way he had? What had he hoped to achieve by involving Emma in such a convoluted way? If she hadn't been his mistress, then why give her half of his estate? What possible reason could he have had for doing such a thing?

His father hadn't known Emma before she came to look after him. She had been a total stranger to him and yet he had tied things up to her advantage, giving her the trump card, leaving his only remaining heir at her mercy. Had his father known how he would react? Had he planned this? Why had he used an innocent girl to get back at his estranged son?

Rafaele carefully lifted himself off her, his insides twisting with guilt as he saw a smear of her blood on his body. His throat felt raw and tight and he inwardly grimaced as she hastily tried to cover herself, her face aflame, her grey-blue eyes looking wounded.

He handed her the shorts and top she had taken off earlier before stepping into his own. 'I am sorry, Emma,' he said heavily. 'I had no idea. I wish you had told me.'

She scrambled back into her shorts and top, her bra and knickers scrunched up in her hand, her eyes shying away from his. 'It's not your fault,' she said. 'I shouldn't have let things go that far…I don't know what came over me…I'm deeply ashamed…'

Rafaele touched her on the arm, his gut clenching again as she flinched away as if she found his touch abhorrent. His hand fell back to his side. 'Do not be ashamed,' he said. 'It was my fault, in any case. I have done nothing but pressure you into having an affair with me. I have no excuse, other than I truly believed you to have seduced my father in order to get your hands on his estate. I can see now I have done you a great disservice. I would not blame you if you walked out right here and now. It is exactly what I deserve.'

She lifted her gaze to his. 'I'm not going to walk out on you,' she said. 'This is your home, Rafaele.'

He scraped a hand through his hair, not at all surprised to see it was still shaking slightly when he brought it back to his side. 'Did my father know you were a virgin?' he asked.

She blushed to the roots of her hair. 'No, of course not! Why would I tell him something like that?'

He gave her a wry look. 'Why indeed?'

Her mouth flattened crossly. 'I had no idea when I came downstairs this morning that we would…you know…'

'Come on, Emma,' he said with a touch of impatience fuelled by his lingering guilt. 'You came down here this morning with every intention of handing me pity on a plate with you served as a garnish.'

'That's not true!' she said. 'I wanted to clear the air between us, that's all.'

He hooked one brow up sceptically. 'That was some flag of friendship you were waving,' he said. 'Do you kiss all of your friends like that?'

She gave him a brittle glare. 'You started it. You kissed me first.'

'Ah, yes, but then you stuck your hand down my shorts,' he said with a twisted, humourless smile. 'That is going a little further than friendship, I would have thought.'

Her cheeks were fiery red, her eyes flashing with sparks of irritation. 'Do you have to rub it in?' she asked. 'I told you I'm thoroughly ashamed of myself. I can't believe I acted like that. I lost control completely, but I can assure you it won't happen again.'

'Pity,' he said. 'I was just starting to enjoy myself.'

Emma drew in a prickly breath. 'Don't make me feel any worse than I already do,' she said. 'I realise it must have been…uncomfortable for you…to be left like…like that…'

'You mean unsatisfied?' he asked.

Her throat went up and down. 'Yes…I suppose that's what I do mean…'

'Put it out of your mind,' he reassured her. 'I am not going to die because I didn't get my rocks off. I can handle a bit of frustration now and again.'

'Yes, well, I'm sure it doesn't happen very often,' Emma said with a little pang of errant jealousy.

'No, not if I can help it,' he said. 'But then boys will be boys, eh, Emma?'

Emma wondered if he was mocking her again. The differences between them had never been more apparent. He was a cynical, experienced playboy who took pleasure how and where he wanted, while she was a romantic fool in search of a home-and-hearth-happy-ever-after. 'Are you laughing at me?' she asked.

He stroked a finger down the length of her cheek. 'Why would I do that, Emma?' he asked, looking at her with those darker-than-night, unreadable eyes.

Emma felt her spine start to unhinge. 'You probably think I'm an old-fashioned prig,' she said. 'Someone who hasn't lived life at all.'

'I do not think that at all,' he said with a little frown beetling his brows.

'I know I'm far too old to be without experience, but I haven't found anyone I liked enough to take that step,' she said. 'I wanted to be in love with the person first. I didn't want it to be just a physical thing.'

His frown deepened. 'So why did you let me make love to you just then?' he asked.

Emma felt her colour rise again as his probing gaze held hers. 'I-I'm not sure…'

The line of his mouth tightened. 'So it *was* just a pity lay,' he said crudely. 'I guessed as much.'

'That's not true,' she said, biting her lip again.

He moved away from her, his expression locking her out once more. 'It will not happen again,' he said, unwittingly driving a stake through her heart. 'It *must not* happen again.'

Her throat closed over until she could barely speak. 'If that's what you want…'

His eyes clashed with hers, pain glittering in their ink-black depths. 'Do you know what I want, Emma? *Do you?*'

She shook her head, fresh tears suddenly blurring her vision.

'I want my life back,' he bit out as he raked a hand through his already tussled hair. 'I want to start over. I want to pick up that cricket ball and throw it into the pond instead of towards my brother's raised bat.' He took in a breath and added hollowly, 'And I want to rewind the clock to the day before my mother died so I could have told her how much I loved her while I still had the chance.'

Emma choked back a sob as he continued in the same bitter, heart-wrenching tone, 'I do not even know if I ever told her that I loved her. Everyone throws those three little words around so casually these days, but I do not remember if I did or not. I was only six years old at the time. If I did I have never said those words since, not to anyone.'

'You can't shut off your feelings for ever,' she said. 'I am sure you are more than capable of loving someone. I am sure of it.'

He drew in a ragged breath. 'I am sorry for what happened here this morning, truly sorry,' he said. 'I must have some sort of curse on me; all I seem to do is wreck people's lives.'

'You haven't wrecked my life,' Emma said softly.

'I hurt you.' He gave her an agonised look. 'I made you bleed, for God's sake.'

'I'm fine…really I am,' she said.

'Maybe you should see a doctor to make sure…'

'That would be embarrassing and totally unnecessary,' Emma insisted. 'Really, Rafaele, please don't cut yourself up about it. It was bound to happen some time or other, if not with you then someone else.'

He came back to where she was standing and, reaching out with one of his hands, gently brushed her hair back off her forehead with a touch so tender Emma felt as if someone had placed an industrial-sized clamp on her heart. He didn't say anything; he just stood there with his eyes holding hers, his thumb moving in a rhythmic fashion against the softness of her cheek.

'I'm glad it was you, Rafaele…' she told him in a whisper-soft voice.

His hand dropped away from her face. 'Why?'

She drew in a little hitching breath. 'Because you made me feel things I have never felt before.'

Pain flickered briefly in his eyes. 'Do not make this any harder than it already is for me, Emma,' he said. 'You are young and far too inexperienced for someone like me.'

'Why do you say that?' she asked.

'I say it because it is true,' he said. 'This attraction I feel for you will burn itself out in no time at all. It always has with everyone else I have been involved with. It is the thrill of the chase. It is a primal urge that all men feel, some more than others.'

'If I wasn't so inexperienced would you be pushing me away right now?' she asked.

'If I thought you were developing feelings for me, then, yes, I would push you away, for your own good.'

Emma felt another piece of her heart crack. 'Isn't it up to me to decide what is good or not good for me?' she asked.

His dark eyes flashed at her angrily. 'Stop this, Emma. Stop it right now. It is not going to go any further than this. It should not have gone this far, damn it to hell.'

Tears began to course down her face and she scrubbed at them with a jerky movement of her hand. 'Do you hate me so much?' she asked.

He swore under his breath and reached for her, pulling her into his chest, bringing his chin down to rest on the top of her head. 'No, no, no, *mio piccolo*,' he said huskily. 'Maybe before…but not now…not now…'

Emma nestled closer, her cheek pressed against the deep thudding of his heart. 'Then…then can we be friends?'

His hand continued stroking the back of her head as if he

wasn't quite ready to release her. But after a moment or two he eased her away from his chest to look down at her uptilted face. 'You are a sweet person, Emma,' he said. 'Anyone would be proud to have a friend as caring and giving as you.'

Emma rose up on tiptoe and pressed a brush-like kiss to his lips. 'Thank you for saying that. I think it's the nicest thing you've ever said to me.'

He grimaced ruefully. 'Yes, well, I have not exactly been handing out the compliments to you, now, have I?'

She smiled up at him. 'So we got off to a bad start? That doesn't mean we can't forgive and forget.'

Something came and went in his dark eyes. 'I can handle the forgiving part, Emma,' he said. 'It is the forgetting that is the most difficult. I do not know if I will ever be able to do it.'

'You are too hard on yourself,' she said. 'If things had been the other way around, would you have wanted your brother to punish himself the way you have punished yourself?'

He looked down at her for a long moment. 'No, you are right. I would not expect him to do so. It was an accident, a tragic accident that might not have happened a second or even half a second later.'

'I think your father came to that conclusion too,' she said. 'He must have thought about how he had handled things and at the last minute realised how wrong he had been.'

'But why involve you?' he asked as he released her from his light hold. 'What did he hope to achieve by that?'

Emma wrinkled her brow. 'I don't know… We might never find out why. Sometimes that's just the way it is. There is no clear-cut explanation for why people do the things they do. But I feel very strongly he would not have left his estate to both of us if he didn't think we could be of help to each other in some way.'

He gave her another rueful look. 'I have not exactly been

much help to you so far, have I? I have torn strips off you at every opportunity, and then to add insult to injury I have robbed you of an experience that should have been precious and memorable, and turned it into a disgusting display of out-of-control male lust, hurting you in the process.' He shouldered open the door and added bitterly, 'I will never forgive myself for that and neither will I forget it.'

Emma winced as the door clicked shut behind him. *I will never forget it either*, she thought, and, once she was certain he was out of earshot, burst into tears.

CHAPTER NINE

WHEN Emma came downstairs that evening for dinner, Carla the new temporary housekeeper informed her in fractured English that Signore Fiorenza would not be joining her as he had been called away on business and would be away for the rest of the week. Emma did her best not to show her disappointment, but inside she felt crushed that Rafaele hadn't bothered to tell her about his trip face to face. What the housekeeper made of the relayed message, Emma didn't like to think. She had already seen Carla's raised brow when she had come out of the Pink Suite that morning. The housekeeper had clearly thought it rather strange the brand-new bride of Rafaele Fiorenza did not choose to share his bed at night.

'Thank you, Carla,' Emma said and, pushing aside her pride, asked: 'Did he happen to mention where he was going?'

'London,' the housekeeper said. 'I think he has a…how you say it in English…a mansion there?'

'Yes, that is correct,' Emma said. 'A mansion.' *And a mistress*, she added in silent anguish.

'I will serve you dinner now.' Carla gave a little bow of her head.

'It's all right, Carla,' Emma said. 'I can fend for myself this evening. You've had a long day as it is. Please take the rest of the night off.'

The housekeeper wavered uncertainly. 'Are you sure, Signora Fiorenza?'

Emma stretched her lips into a tight smile. 'Yes, I'm very sure. I'm not very hungry, in any case. I think I'll have an early night.'

'As you wish,' Carla said, and with a polite nod backed away.

Emma blew out a long sigh once the housekeeper had left. Rafaele couldn't have chosen a better way to communicate how much he regretted their passionate interlude that morning. He obviously wanted to put as much distance as he could between them so he wouldn't be tempted into finishing what he had started. She cringed as she recalled his statement that his attraction for her was just a transitory thing that would soon burn itself out. Could he so easily dismiss what they had shared?

Emma couldn't. She could still feel an intimate ache inside where her untried muscles had been called into sudden play. Thinking about his thick, hard body filling hers made her body fizz with sensation, as if sherbet instead of blood were flowing through her veins. Recalling the feel of his naked flesh under her fingertips, the tantalising taste of his kiss and the cup of his warm hands on her breasts made her need for him so intense, a giant hole opened in the pit of her stomach. He had awakened her to needs she had barely known existed. Those needs were now suspended, unsatisfied and all the stronger because they had been roused to fever pitch.

Emma swung away from her thoughts and made her way back up the stairs, coming to a halt outside Rafaele's brother's room, and with just a moment's hesitation she opened the door and stepped inside.

The bed had been pushed up against the wall and several boxes were now in the middle of the floor, some with toys and books, and others with clothes and shoes as Rafaele had begun the painful process of packing away his younger brother's things.

Emma bent down and picked up a rather tattered-looking teddy bear sitting on the top of the box of toys, the brown velvet pads of his paws almost worn away where little fingers had stroked, perhaps looking for night-time comfort. She felt tears welling at the backs of her eyes for the little boy who had been in the right place at the wrong time, and for Rafaele who had had to live each day since with a sinkhole of guilt and despair in his soul.

She tucked the teddy bear close to her chest, deciding that this little guy wasn't going to the charity shop or the attic or wherever else Rafaele intended the rest of Giovanni's things to go.

On her way to bed a couple of hours later, Emma had more or less given up on Rafaele calling her, but the telephone next to her bed suddenly began to ring so she picked it up and answered it somewhat tentatively. *'Buongiorno?'*

'Emma.'

Emma felt her spine shiver at the sound of her name on Rafaele's lips. 'Oh…it's you…' she said, injecting each word with some of her hurt at being abandoned so readily.

'Are you OK?' he asked.

'Yes.'

'You do not sound it.'

'Then you are imagining things,' she said. 'I'm fine.'

'Emma…' she heard him pull in a breath '…I had to leave in a hurry. Something came up, something urgent. I had to catch the first available flight to London to sort it out.'

'You could have told me yourself instead of getting the housekeeper to do so,' Emma said. 'I felt such a fool. We're supposed to be acting like a married couple, remember?'

'I am sorry you were embarrassed but—'

Emma cut across him in frustration. 'Married couples are supposed to talk to each other. It's called communication.'

There was a tense little pause.

'Emma, I would have told you personally but you were lying down in your room. I did not wish to disturb you.'

'How do you know I was lying down?' she asked.

'I knocked on your door and when you didn't answer I opened it,' he said. 'You were sound asleep.'

Emma felt a faint shiver pass over her at the thought of him observing her without her knowing. 'You should have woken me up.'

'You looked exhausted, that is why I didn't,' he said. 'I was in a rush, in any case.'

'You could have phoned me once you were on your way in the car or even at the airport,' she said, not quite ready to relinquish her sense of pique. 'Why didn't you?'

He let out an impatient sound. 'Must we have this conversation?' he asked. 'I didn't realise you expected me to clock in and clock out.'

'I'm sure that's what you expect me to do,' she threw back resentfully. 'I bet if I left some vague message with the housekeeper or one of the groundsmen that I was going away for the best part of a week you would have something to say about it.'

'I would indeed,' he said, 'but that is because you are my wife and I will not have my reputation damaged by inappropriate behaviour on your part.'

Emma felt her anger towards him escalate. 'I'm hardly the one in this marriage to act inappropriately, now, am I?'

'What is that supposed to mean?' He bit each word out like small hard pebbles hitting against a glass surface.

'I'm n-not the one with a lover in every city throughout

Europe,' she said, struggling to keep her voice steady as her emotions started to bubble over. 'That's you.'

'Emma, you are overwrought,' he said in a gentler tone. 'It is understandable given what happened this morning. That is one of the reasons I came away when I did. I think we both need some space to regroup.'

Emma bit down on her lip to stop herself from crying.

'Emma?' he said. '*Cara*, listen to me…please.'

She gave a tell-tale little sniff. 'S-sorry…it's just I don't know what you want from me…'

Rafaele closed his eyes and with his free hand used his finger and thumb to pinch the bridge of his nose until he winced at the pressure.

What *did* he want from her? Something he had no right to ask of her. She was after security and safety and he was not the one to give it to her. He didn't trust himself. He had never been good at relationships. He got restless and bored within weeks of sleeping with a new partner. It happened every single time. It would not be fair to have an affair with her, only to walk away when the curtain came down on the year required to fulfil the terms of his father's will.

He had misjudged her so badly he couldn't bear to add insult to injury by offering her a convenient affair. She deserved so much better. She deserved to have someone who could love her and protect her, to nurture her and meet all her needs. It would pull her down to have someone like him in her life. He couldn't give her the children she wanted. *How could he?* What sort of father would he be? He didn't feel comfortable around children. The nightmares never went away. He would wake up in his bed, soaked in sweat, his heart thumping, and his mind filled with images of his brother lying lifeless on the ground.

'Emma…' He took a deep breath and continued, 'It was

not my intention to confuse you. But everything is different now. It has to be.'

'But what about what I want?' she asked.

Rafaele's fingers tensed around his phone. 'I cannot give you what you want.'

'How do you *know* that?'

He blew out another tight breath. 'I just know it. I am not the settling down type. You told me you wanted a proper love-match marriage and children eventually. That is just not going to happen with me.'

'Because you're still punishing yourself,' she said. 'You're robbing yourself of one of the richest experiences in life.'

'My father clearly did not find it so,' he reminded her bitterly.

'Your father was as stubborn and proud as you,' she said. 'But have you ever thought what it was like for him losing your mother so young? He was probably devastated, left with two little boys to rear. One of the guests at the wedding told me he had loved your mother since childhood. Can't you imagine how lost he must have felt when she died so unexpectedly?'

Rafaele frowned and changed his phone to his other hand, flexing his fingers to ease the tension, but it crawled up from his hand to stiffen his neck instead. 'He did not talk about my mother,' he said. 'Not once in all the years after her death. He was the same with Giovanni. The day of my brother's funeral was the last time I heard Giovanni's name mentioned by him.'

'And yet he kept Giovanni's room as he had left it for all these years,' she said softly. 'And your mother's wedding dress was as perfect as the day she had worn it and the room she had decorated all by herself untouched. Can't you see how deeply he must have still been grieving? Perhaps he was just unable to express it the way you expected him to.'

Rafaele felt a growing ache in the region of his heart, like a very large hand reaching inside his chest and slowly squeezing. He couldn't speak for a moment as his throat was so tight. How would he ever know now what his father had thought and felt? Emma was right about him being as stubborn as his father. Over the past decade he could easily have made an effort to make contact, but he had been too pigheaded to do so. He had told himself he didn't want to see that look of loathing on his father's face ever again. The months and years had rolled by and now it was too late.

'Rafaele?'

He gave himself a mental shake as Emma's soft voice pierced his painful thoughts. 'This is not a good time for me, Emma,' he said. 'I have hours of work ahead of me. I will call you in a day or two.'

There was a stiff little silence.

'Are you seeing her?'

He frowned. 'Seeing who?'

'Your mistress.'

Rafaele waited for a two-beat pause. 'I no longer have a mistress. I told you I ended that relationship before we got married.'

'But we're not really married, are we, Rafaele?' she said. 'You don't want it to be real because you would rather have the freedom to see other women whenever you want.'

'I am not seeing anyone at present,' he said. 'Now, please stop this nonsense before I lose all patience with you.'

She couldn't stop. She was so frustrated she had to keep going. 'If you're going to have a lover on the side I think I should be allowed to do the same.'

Jealousy rose like a red-hot lava flow inside Rafaele at her defiant statement. He had never felt anything quite like the force of it before. The thought of her young and tender, un-tutored body being taken by someone else made him sick to his stomach. What if they were too rough with her as—God forgive him—he had been? She needed to be gently and patiently initiated into the rhythm of lovemaking, not rushed or pressured.

Rafaele suddenly realised *he* wanted to be the one to show her the pleasure her body could give and receive. His body was still humming with the sensations her touch had evoked that morning. He could still taste her sweetness in his mouth, he could still feel the softness of her lips and he could still feel the satin and silk of her naked breasts against his hands.

'No,' he stated implacably. 'I will not allow you to take a lover.'

'I'm not asking for your permission, Rafaele,' she said in an arch tone.

Rafaele ground his teeth as he pulled his anger back into line. 'The only lover you will be taking during our marriage will be me, do you understand, Emma? No one else. Just me.'

'But you said—'

'I know what I said but I have changed my mind,' he interrupted her curtly. 'When I return to Como our marriage will be a real one in every sense of the word. Get the housekeeper to help you move your things into my room. I want you in my bed when I get home.'

Emma felt a frisson run up her spine at his toe-curling command. Her body came alive, every place he had touched or caressed that morning started to quake with longing, the nerves beneath her skin leaping and bouncing in anticipation. Her breasts felt tight and full and her inner muscles gave a couple of tiny contraction-like pulses as if already preparing for the invasion of his aroused length. Desire flowed thickly through her veins, making her almost giddy with it. Her heart picked up its pace, her skin peppering with fine beads of perspiration as she tried to control the in-and-out of her choppy breathing.

'Did you hear me, Emma?' he asked in that same commanding tone.

'Y-yes…I heard you…'

'Non aver paura, mio piccolo,' he said in a deep but gentle voice. 'Do not be frightened, my little one. I will not hurt you the next time.'

Emma's belly did a little freefall of excitement. 'When are you coming home?' she asked.

'I would come on the next flight if I could, *cara*, but I am afraid that is impossible,' he said. 'I really do have urgent business to see to. There is a rather large share portfolio I am interested in. I am meeting with the chief executive of the company in a few hours. If all goes well I will be home on Saturday evening. Can you wait for me until then?'

Emma suddenly felt wretchedly ashamed at how she had practically begged him to come home to her. She had come across as a wanton, desperate for sex, blackmailing him with the threat of another lover to bed her. What full-blooded man wouldn't take her up on her offer? It wasn't about feelings on his part, or at least not emotional ones. It was about sex. A purely physical need that could be met with any number of women, but she in her naivety had put her hand up the highest.

Emma mentally cringed at her clumsy attempt at seduction. She was such a novice. Had she forgotten why he had married her in the first place? He wanted The Villa Fiorenza, not her. She was the annoying caveat his father had attached to his will. All she had to do to confirm it was to ask him how long he wanted their marriage to continue.

Go on, the sensible part of her brain urged, *ask him. Ask him if he wants to stay married beyond the year set down in the will.*

Emma couldn't do it. She didn't want to know. Why torture herself with a timeline? What good would it do to spend each day ticking off the calendar, another piece of her heart breaking beyond repair as the inevitable end approached?

'Emma?'

His deep velvet-toned voice jerked her back into the moment. 'Um…you don't have to hurry back if you're busy.' She faltered. 'I understand you have a business to run and…and people to see.'

'I would much prefer to see you than an overweight CEO, but that is just the way it is for now, *mio piccolo*.'

Emma wished that niggling voice in her head would go away. She desperately wanted to believe him, but her doubts kept sneaking up and tapping her on the shoulder long after she had put the phone down after saying goodbye.

The next few days passed so slowly Emma felt as if lead weights had been strapped to the hands of the clock. Each minute seemed to limp past, making her feel uncharacteristically restless and edgy.

Emma had not yet moved her things into Rafaele's suite. It seemed such a huge step to take, to occupy his bed while he wasn't there as if they had a normal relationship. Nothing about their marriage was normal. She had a ring on her finger and a certificate that declared them legally married, but Rafaele still had a chip on his shoulder about his father and until that was resolved she didn't think he would ever move on enough to allow her a space in his heart. Her love for him had gradually crept up on her. She hadn't realised how intense her feelings were until she had finally been brave enough to pull back the screen of denial.

Of course she was in love with him.

She hadn't stood a chance under the blowtorch of his bad-boy charm. She had melted like butter, her body recognising from the first moment when they had locked gazes he was the one for her. He was the one man who had sent her senses spinning, turned her world upside down, her bones to liquid and her heart to mush. One look had started it, one smile had encouraged it and one kiss had confirmed it. What would making love to completion with him do to her already out of control emotions?

The housekeeper came in with the papers on the Saturday morning, her expression giving nothing away for free, but Emma sensed a pitying attitude in the way Carla retreated without once meeting her eyes.

Emma soon found the reason why on the gossip pages of one of the British scandal sheets. There was a photograph of Rafaele leaning in close to a gorgeous blonde woman wearing an evening dress slit to the navel, her full-lipped mouth pouting to receive his kiss. Emma closed her eyes and tried to get the image out of her brain, but when she opened them again it was still there, taunting her, reminding her of how stupid she had been to think she had even stood a chance.

The woman's name was Miranda Bellingstoke, a rich heiress to a fortune in stocks and shares, just the type of socialite wife Rafaele Fiorenza would have chosen if his father hadn't interfered. A woman who knew how to carry herself, a woman with a pedigree longer than her perfect, cellulite-free legs, a woman who didn't have a single drug-addicted skeleton in her closet, a woman who knew how to meet his needs and who had no doubt been meeting them the whole time he was in London. The article hinted as much. It speculated how Ms Bellingstoke's involvement with the high-flying Italian stock trader seemed to be on again in spite of his recent marriage to an Australian woman.

Nausea lifted Emma's stomach contents to her throat and she swallowed against it, fighting against the imminent collapse of her spirit. At least the journalist hadn't mentioned

Emma by name, but still the shame of being identified as the poor, ignorant wife, the last to know of her husband's affair, clung to her like filthy mud.

It was more than obvious the 'urgent' business he had to see to was five feet ten and weighed less than Emma did at five feet five. How could she compete against that? Rafaele was used to sophisticated women of the world. He had probably been laughing about her inexperience to his worldly mistress, no doubt relating to her how Emma had prostrated herself, pleading to be shown what it meant to be a woman in passionate command of a man who had so much experience he deserved a doctorate.

Emma felt herself shrinking in shame. How could she have been so dumb? It was obvious now how this was going to pan out. He would travel back and forth to London 'on business' leaving her back at the villa to twiddle her thumbs waiting with bated breath for his return. What better revenge for how she had supposedly insinuated her way into his father's affections? He would get exactly what he wanted with a little bonus thrown in.

Her.

But it wasn't going to go all his way, not if she could help it.

She would be more than ready for him when he returned; she would have her resolve hardened, her chin at a combative angle, her heart under lock and key.

Emma heard the low growl of his car a few hours later and straightened her spine as she waited for him to come in. She heard the firm tread of his footsteps on the marbled floors and his voice echoing throughout the large foyer as he called her. '*Cara*, I am home. Where are you, *la mio bella moglie*?'

She walked stiffly out of the salon, her chin held high, her eyes glittering with wrath. 'Here I am,' she said.

His gaze ran over her, a quizzical light in their dark depths. 'Emma, has something happened? You look…tense.'

'How was your business in London?' she asked. 'Satisfying?'

A frown brought his brows together. 'I achieved what I set out to achieve, if that is what you are asking, but somehow I get the feeling it is not. What is going on? Why are you looking at me like that?'

Emma gave him a hard little glare. 'You lied to me. You said your affair with your mistress was over but it's not, is it? I saw you with Miranda Bellingstoke in the paper.'

A flicker of irritation passed over his features. 'I did not lie to you, Emma. I am no longer involved with Miranda.'

Emma clenched her hands into fists. 'But you saw her while you were there, didn't you? There's no point denying it as I saw the photo of you with her in the London paper.'

He sucked in a breath and dragged a hand through his hair. 'All right,' he said with a hint of weariness. 'I did see her, but not intentionally. The CEO I was dealing with suggested we have a drink once we had sorted out the business end of things. Miranda happened to be at the same bar.'

Emma rolled her eyes. 'How very convenient.'

His jaw went tight. 'I did not plan to see her, Emma. She came over to where we were standing at the bar and, if the truth be known, made rather a nuisance of herself.'

'Would you like to see the press's version of Miranda making a nuisance of herself?' Emma asked with a little curl of her lip.

He set his mouth. 'I do not see the need to defend myself to you, Emma,' he said. 'After all, you have experienced the bias of the press first hand, have you not? I would have thought you would be the first person to give me the benefit of the doubt.'

Emma could see his point, but still those little finger-prod doubts kept nudging her. She felt so confused. He was a playboy. He was used to his freedom. He had only married her because he'd had no choice. Would she ever feel secure enough to trust him?

He stepped closer and gently lifted her chin so she had to meet his gaze. 'Have you changed your mind about making our marriage a real one?' he asked.

Emma looked into his bottomless black-brown eyes and melted. How could she say no to him when she loved him so much? Even if she could only have him for the rest of the year wouldn't that be better than not at all? 'No…' Her voice came out whisper-soft. 'No, I haven't changed my mind.'

He began to stroke her cheek with the pad of his thumb. 'I should have warned you how intrusive the press can be. I do my best to ignore them, but occasionally they go too far.'

She lowered her eyes a fraction. 'I guess I really don't have any right to be jealous…it's not as if we're in love…or anything…'

He looked at her for a second or two. 'No, perhaps not, but no one likes to feel they are being double-crossed.'

Her eyes came back to his. 'So…so while we are…together there won't be anyone else in your life?'

Again he took a moment to answer. 'I suppose we should make some sort of agreement that if one of us develops an interest elsewhere, we should inform the other of it so as to avoid unnecessary embarrassment. How does that sound?'

It sounds as if you are never going to fall in love with me and are making sure you have a quick exit route, Emma thought in silent despair. 'Fine,' she said with a tight smile. 'Best to be up front and honest about these things.'

Rafaele tucked a strand of her hair behind her ear. 'I am going to have a shower and a shave and come back down to the salon and pour us both a drink. Have you eaten?'

'Ages ago, but what about you?'

'I had a snack on the plane but I could do with something light,' he said, tugging at his tie. 'Has Carla left anything for us?'

'I will go and get it ready for you.'

He bent down and pressed a brief kiss to her forehead. 'I have been thinking of nothing else but holding you in my arms and making love to you.'

Emma let out a shuddering breath of anticipation as she looked into his dark eyes. 'I've been thinking about it too…'

He smiled and brushed his mouth against hers in a hot-as-fire-but-soft-as-a-feather kiss that set her heart racing. 'Hold that thought,' he said with a smouldering look. 'I will not be long.'

CHAPTER TEN

WHEN Rafaele came downstairs after his shower Emma had poured a ruby-red glass of wine for him and set a plate of salad and a freshly made omelette on the coffee-table.

'Is Carla still here?' he asked as he sat down and picked up the knife and fork.

'No, I made it myself,' Emma said. 'I thought it would be nicer than reheated pasta.'

'That was kind of you,' he said. 'Are you going to have something? What about a glass of wine? Can I pour you one?'

She shook her head. 'No, I had an orange juice a while ago.'

He resumed eating; pausing now and again to chat to her about the weather in London and other inconsequential things, but Emma only listened with one ear. She drank in the sight of him, the way his mouth tilted at the corners when he smiled and the way his eyes softened when they met hers. He looked tired, but not tense this time. She hoped it was because he was glad to be back at the villa with her.

Rafaele pushed his empty plate aside. 'Come here,' he commanded softly.

Emma got up on unsteady legs and sat beside him on the leather sofa, shivering with delight when his arm came around her shoulders and brought her closer. She looked into his eyes, her heart skipping a beat at the passion she could see burning there.

He brought his mouth down to hers in a slow, sensual kiss that made all the fine hairs on Emma's body stand to attention. His tongue slipped through the soft barrier of her lips and she began to suck on its tip, delighting in the way he groaned with pleasure as he deepened the kiss.

His hands shaped her through her clothes, his mouth still locked on hers, his body pressing hers down on the sofa until she felt the hard length of him probing her intimately.

Rafaele lifted his head and looked down at her passion-swollen lips. 'This is not the place to do this,' he said. 'I want you to be comfortable and relaxed.'

Emma was swept away on a tide of such longing she was hardly aware of Rafaele lifting her and carrying her upstairs to his bedroom. She clung to him, her mouth crushed beneath the pressure of his, her heart rate racing out of control as he laid her on the mattress.

'Are you sure about this, Emma?' he asked as he came down beside her, his warm fingers splayed possessively on her hip. '*Really* sure?'

She looked at him with love shining in her eyes. 'I'm sure,' she said. 'It's what I want. I want you. I want you to make love to me.'

He kissed her mouth, a hard, brief kiss that burned with sensual promise. 'I cannot help feeling I should not be doing this,' he said as he lifted up her T-shirt to expose her breasts.

'But you want to, don't you?' Emma asked, squirming as his mouth began to suckle on her engorged flesh.

'Damn right I do,' he growled, and moved to her other breast. 'I think I have wanted to do this from the moment I met you.'

Emma gasped with pleasure as he moved his mouth down from her breasts to the tiny cave of her belly button, his tongue circling the indentation before moving lower. She automatically tensed but he spoke to her softly, his deep, sexy voice soothing her into relaxing as he subjected her to the most intimate of erotic caresses. Her body quivered, each sensitised nerve beginning to vibrate with pleasure under the exquisite torture of his mouth and tongue.

'Come for me, Emma,' he coaxed her gently.

Emma felt her body start to convulse, it was suddenly out of her control, the waves of rapture swamping her, leaving her breathless and euphoric and even more hopelessly in love.

She stroked her fingers through the thickness of his hair and let out a shaky sigh as the last tremors of pleasure rippled through her. 'I can't believe that just happened...' she said. 'I didn't know it would feel like that...'

Rafaele moved up her body, settling himself between her thighs, one of his legs splayed over one of hers. 'It will get better,' he said. 'It takes time to get used to a new lover. We have to learn each other's rhythm and pace.'

'Teach me how to pleasure you,' she said, tracing the outline of his mouth. 'Teach me everything.'

He brought her hand to his erection, letting her feel his rigid contours, hoping it would help her relax enough to accept him. 'I do not want to hurt you, Emma,' he said. 'It's important you relax as much as possible, don't tense up. I will let you set the pace, just tell me whenever you need me to stop.'

She bit her lip in that endearing way of hers. 'OK...'

He reached past her to take out a condom from the bedside drawer and, opening the tiny packet, handed it to her. 'You can put it on me, if you like.'

She peeled it back over him, the tip of her tongue between her teeth in concentration, her fingers soft and tentative as if worried she might hurt him. He found it a new experience being with someone so caring and sweet and so trusting. He was used to lovers going after what they wanted; the slightly aggressive and raunchy sexuality of modern women had never bothered him before now. Sex for him had been always been a totally physical thing. He had always been perfectly content with that, but now he wondered if he had missed out on something along the way.

He drew in a breath as her fingers began stroking him, the movements so deliciously tantalising he thought he might not last the distance. He pushed her back down, and, propping his weight on his arms, gently lowered his pelvis to hers. He touched her delicate folds, the sweet honey of her body slick against his fingers. 'Remember, Emma,' he said. 'Any time you want to stop, just tell me.'

'I don't want you to stop,' she said a little breathlessly.

He stroked her some more, inserting one then two fingers, letting her grip and then relax around him until he pushed deeper. 'You feel so wet and warm and tight,' he said, fighting for control.

'I want you inside me,' she said, shifting her body restively beneath him. 'I want you inside me now.'

He smiled over her mouth as he bent to kiss it. 'Don't be so impatient, *cara*,' he said. 'There is plenty of time. We have got all night.'

She kissed him back, her tongue tangling with his, her breathing coming in little gasps as he prepared to enter her. He took it very slowly, easing into her tight warmth until he felt she was ready for more of him. Bit by bit he advanced, his senses spinning as her small body enclosed him, the feel of her around his thickness making him want to selfishly plunge in and explode. It took every gram of patience and control to hold back, he could feel the pressure building inside him; he was almost shuddering with the effort of holding back, his skin breaking out in fine beads of perspiration as he coaxed her into accepting his full length.

She tensed momentarily at one point and he instantly eased back, and, propping himself up again, brushed the damp hair away from her forehead. 'How are you doing?' he asked.

'I'm fine...I think I'm fine now...'

He pushed in a bit further. 'You feel so good, Emma,' he said.

Emma pushed her hips up to take more of him, her mouth on his neck in hot little kisses that spoke of her own building need. He sucked in a harsh breath and began to gently thrust, the rocking motion sending her senses into a tailspin. Her skin was peppered with goose-bumps of pleasure as he increased the pace; she was with him all the way, her body so slick with moisture she could feel nothing but the smooth, hard glide of his body within the tight cocoon of hers. Her body began to fizz and tingle with each deepening thrust, her back arching, her legs stiffening in that prelude to paradise. She was so close but not quite there when he brought his fingers into play against her, the gentle but purposeful action intensifying the tight coils of pleasure until they suddenly unravelled, leaving her shuddering and quaking and sobbing her way through an explosive, earth-shattering orgasm.

Emma lay beneath him, her body still quivering as she felt him prepare for his own release. She felt it in the growing tension of his muscles on his back where her fingers were still digging into him, and she felt it in the way his pace began to step up, the pumping action of his body as it thrust into hers signalling he was getting closer and closer to that final blissful moment. He surged forwards, the quake of his body as he spilled himself sending her skin out in another layer of pimply goose-flesh, her body feeling every single shuddering pulse of his.

The silence was measured by the sound of their hectic breathing. Emma closed her eyes and breathed in the musky scent of their lovemaking, her senses still spinning at the heady pleasure she had felt in his arms. His body was heavy on hers, but she didn't want him to move. She loved the feel of him relaxed and spent on top of her, his face buried against her neck, the in and out of his breathing feathering along her sensitive skin.

'You were amazing, Emma,' he said, the movement of his lips against her skin making her shiver in reaction.

'So were you,' she responded shyly.

He leaned up on his elbows to look down at her, his brows close together over his eyes. 'Did I hurt you?' he asked.

Emma shook her head. 'Not much… A little at first but you were so gentle with me.' She smiled and lifted herself up to plant a soft kiss on his mouth. 'Thank you.'

He returned her kiss with a lingering one of his own. 'You are welcome,' he said, and carefully lifted himself off her, discarding the condom in the process.

He pulled her to her feet and held her against him for a moment, his hands resting on her hips, their bodies touching pelvis to pelvis. Emma felt the stirring of him against her and pressed herself closer, but he held her from him with a rueful smile. 'No, Emma,' he said. 'You will be too sore.'

Emma had to dampen down her disappointment. Her body was on fire all over again and she didn't want anything to spoil their new-found harmony, even if it was only physical. 'What if we have a shower together?' she asked, looping her arms around his neck.

His eyes flared with desire as he looked down at her. 'You ask too much,' he said in a mock growl. 'Do you think I will be able to control myself with you splashing around naked beside me?'

She gave him a coquettish smile. 'I could always put on a bathing costume if that would help?'

'Don't you dare,' he growled and, sweeping her up in his arms, carried her through to the *en suite*.

The fine needles of water were hot and caressing against Emma's skin, but nowhere near as caressing as Rafaele's dark brown gaze as it ran over every inch of her. Everywhere his gaze rested her body sprang to zinging life, her mouth, her breasts, the flat plane of her stomach and lower to where her feminine mound was already contracting with growing need.

'I knew this would be a mistake,' he murmured against her neck as he nibbled at her sensitive skin, his hands splayed on her bottom, holding her against his arousal. 'But I can't seem to help myself. You are driving me crazy. You have been doing it from day one.'

Emma tilted her head so she could feel his lips and tongue near the base of her ear. 'I like how you make me feel,' she said, clutching at his broad shoulders. 'I didn't know my body could feel the things you make it feel.'

'You make me feel some amazing things as well,' he said, and kissed her on the mouth, his tongue delving deep as his lower body rubbed against hers, the rough abrasion of his hair-roughened skin making her desire for him all the more uncontrollable.

Emma trailed her fingers from his neck, down his chest, circling his flat brown nipples before going lower to where his erection pulsed and throbbed with longing. She sank to her knees in the cubicle, the steamy water cascading over her shoulders and back as she brought her mouth towards him.

His fingers dug into her scalp to hold her at bay. 'You don't have to do that, Emma,' he said a little breathlessly. 'That is a big ask for a new lover, especially an inexperienced one.'

She looked up at him. 'But I want to pleasure you. I want to know how to make you feel the way I did when you did it to me.'

He brushed the wet hair back off her face. 'I don't want you to do anything you are not comfortable with,' he said. 'I can pull out before things go too far.'

Emma took an unsteady breath, her hands grasping his thighs as she brought her mouth to him, breathing over him first before she tasted him tentatively with the tip of her tongue. She felt him jerk back in response, his fingers digging even further into her hair as he tried to anchor himself against the sensual onslaught to come. It gave her all the confidence she so very badly needed. She licked at him like a hungry cat, her tongue discovering his rigid contours: the thickened shaft with its satin-like skin stretched to snapping point, the musky scent of his arousal filling her nostrils, the pulse of his blood thrumming against the sweep of her tongue.

'Oh, God,' he groaned, beginning to sag at the knees. 'I can't take much more of this.'

Emma kept at him, her mouth sliding over his engorged length, back and forth in a purely instinctive fashion until she felt him suddenly tense, his whole body locking in that pivotal moment when control finally slipped out of reach. She felt the convulsing shudders of his body; she received the spill of his life force, the warmth of him anointing her in one of the most intimate acts possible.

He pulled out of her mouth with a muttered expletive and hauled her almost roughly to her feet. 'You did not have to do that, Emma,' he said. 'I do not want you to feel you have to bend over backwards to please me all the time. We are supposed to be equals.'

'We can only be equals if you come to care for me as much as I care for you,' she said, sliding her hands over his rock-hard pectoral muscles, her eyes gazing into his. 'I love you.'

He frowned at her, his body going tense. 'Emma…' He gave a little sigh and continued, 'You are confusing love with sexual desire. In the first rush of attraction it is an easy mistake to make. Believe me, what you are feeling now will peter out over time.'

'I don't believe that,' Emma said. 'This is not just sexual attraction. *I love you.*'

'A lot of women develop strong feelings for their first lover,' he said. 'You have waited longer than most so it is natural you would form a stronger attachment than normal, but it does not mean it is the real deal.'

'How can I convince you it is?' she asked.

He let out another heavy sigh as he ran his hands from her shoulders down to her wrists. 'I do not want you to love me, Emma,' he said. 'I do not want to be responsible for your unhappiness. I am not good at relationships. I do not like hurting people, but at times it is inevitable. I am selfish and pigheaded and enjoy my freedom too much. Let's just enjoy this while it lasts.'

'How can you not want to be loved?' she asked as she fought back tears. 'What is the point in living if no one loves you?'

'Stop it, Emma,' he said brusquely as he reached past her to turn off the shower spray. 'I told you the rules. I would appreciate it if you would stick to them.'

Emma followed him out of the shower, her heart contracting at his keep-away-from-me manner. He had just made love to her with such exquisite tenderness. Didn't that mean he felt at least something for her?

No, she reminded herself painfully. It did not.

She wrapped herself in a towel and turned away from him in case he saw the distress she felt. How could she have been so foolish? She had blurted out her feelings so gauchely. No wonder he had pulled away. She cringed at her lack of sophistication. Hot, scalding shame rushed through her again at how she had begged him to make love to her like the sex-starved singleton she was.

'Emma,' Rafaele said as he touched her on the shoulder. 'Look at me.'

Emma stiffened under his touch. 'Leave it, Rafaele,' she said without facing him. 'Please don't make me feel any more of a fool than I already do.'

He tugged her around to face him, his hands going to her waist to hold her steady, and his eyes locking on hers. 'I want you, Emma,' he said. 'Make no mistake about that. I want you.'

But not for ever, Emma thought with a little sag of her shoulders as his mouth came down. She gave herself up to his kiss, her arms going around his waist, holding her to him tightly, wondering even as she felt his body quiver with longing against hers how long it would be before he tired of her and finally let her go.

Emma woke up alone the next morning, but when she turned her head she could see where Rafaele's had been resting on the pillow beside hers. She reached out and touched the indention, her nostrils flaring to take in the fragrance of their lovemaking lingering on the sheets. She moved her body experimentally, the tiny tug of her inner muscles reminding her of the mind-blowing passion they had shared during the night. He had been so tender and considerate she had felt tears come to her eyes. Her love for him felt as if it were taking up all the available space inside her chest. She felt it pulling on her every breath with a bittersweet poignancy.

The door of the bedroom pushed open and Rafaele came in bearing a tray with freshly brewed coffee, fruit and croissants. 'Rise and shine,' he said with a smile. 'Breakfast is here.'

Emma dragged herself upright and blinked the sleep out of her eyes. 'What is it about morning people who think everyone should be awake and fully functioning at dawn?' she asked with a mock scowl.

He grinned at her as he laid the tray across her knees. 'Do you need a wake-up kiss, Emma?' he asked, and, leaning forward, pressed his mouth to hers, the brush stroke of his tongue setting her senses alight.

He pulled back and looked at her for a moment. 'Mmm, I am thinking the coffee is too hot in any case,' he said, and lifted the tray off her knees and set it on the floor.

'What are you doing?' Emma asked as he began to haul his T-shirt over his head.

He gave her a burning look and reached for the zipper of his jeans. 'What do you think I am doing?' he asked.

'It looks like you're getting undressed,' she said, and suppressed a little shiver as he stepped out of his jeans. She could see the tenting of his underwear and her heart began to race as he came towards her.

He pulled the sheets off her in a ruthless fashion, his dark gaze feeding off her hungrily. 'You look more beautiful every time I see you,' he said.

'My hair's a mess,' Emma said breathlessly as he came down on top of her.

'It looks wonderful to me,' he said against her mouth. 'You look like you have spent the night making wild, passionate love.'

She squirmed with delight as his erection probed her intimately. 'That's because I did spend the night making wild, passionate love,' she said with a coy little smile.

He eased his weight off her. 'Are you sore?'

'A tiny bit,' she said. 'But it's a nice sore.'

His eyes went very dark as they held hers. 'Maybe I should leave this until later,' he said.

Emma grasped at his shoulders to stop him pulling back from her. 'No, don't you dare,' she said. 'You kissed me so now you'll have to finish what you started.'

His eyes glinted. 'So it's like that, is it?'

She stroked her fingers down to where his body pulsed. 'Yes, it is,' she said, pushing aside his underwear.

He sucked in a breath and pushed her back down to the mattress. 'You're a fast learner, *la mio bella moglie*,' he growled playfully.

'Yes, but then you're a great teacher.' Emma gasped as his mouth closed over her breast, her senses spinning as he circled her nipple with his tongue.

He moved to her other breast with the same exquisite caresses, his hand sliding down to explore her tender folds, making her toes curl in delight.

'I want you inside me,' she said, opening her thighs even further, her hands searching for him to guide him into her slick warmth.

She watched with bated breath as he applied a condom, his body so aroused she could see the veins rippling along the shaft.

He came back over her, his weight supported by his elbows as he looked down at her. 'I should have asked this earlier, but are you on the pill?'

Emma hesitated for a nanosecond. She had begun taking a low-dose pill a few months ago to help control her cycle, but she had not always been very vigilant in taking it. She would have to see a doctor to get a new prescription, in any case.

'Emma?'

'Yes,' she said, promising herself she would make an appointment with a doctor as soon as possible. 'I take it to keep my periods regular.'

He searched her features for an infinitesimal moment. 'I do not want any accidents,' he said. 'Condoms can some-times break.'

'There won't be any accidents,' she said. 'I'm safe.'

He held her gaze for another moment or two. 'Just to reassure you, I had tests done recently,' he said. 'You will not catch anything from me.'

Emma hated being reminded of his playboy lifestyle. She

felt as if she was just a number in a long line of women who had briefly occupied his bed. She knew as soon as he was finished with her someone else would step up and take her place. It was gut-wrenching to think he might only be using her in order to secure his inheritance, but her love for him demanded she spend what little time she had with him to show him how genuine her feelings were. What else could she do? She was locked here with him for the next few months. It would be unbearable if she had to watch on the sidelines while he conducted an affair with someone else.

'I'm glad to hear it,' she said a little stiffly.

'What's wrong?'

'Nothing's wrong.'

He captured her chin to stop her from turning her head away. 'Yes, there is,' he said. 'You are jealous.'

She gave him a glittering glare. 'Why should I be jealous?' she asked. 'You've been very open about the fact you've slept with hundreds of women.'

He gave her a wry look. 'Hardly hundreds.'

'How many, then?' she asked.

He frowned at her darkly. 'I am not going to give you a list of names and numbers, Emma. They have nothing to do with us.'

'Us?' She elevated her brows. 'That's hardly a word to describe you and me, is it? We're not a couple in the real sense of the word. We're only together because we were forced into it.'

'You do not think what happened yesterday makes us a couple?' he asked.

'It was sex, Rafaele. Even strangers have sex; it doesn't make them a couple.'

'We *are* a couple, Emma,' he said. 'I want you to be my lover for as long as we are happy together.'

Emma wished she had the strength of will to get out now before she got her heart broken, but her body was already responding to his thick, hard presence. She dug her fingers into his taut buttocks to bring him deeper, her breath coming in choppy gasps as he began an erotic rhythm. Her nerves began to hum with tension, her body feeling as if a hundred earthquakes were about to erupt inside her. The pressure built in every muscle of her body until she was teetering on the edge, finally pitching forwards into blissful oblivion.

She felt him come close behind her, his body tense and hard before it pumped its way into paradise, his arms tight around her, his face pressed into her neck as he cut back a harsh groan of ecstasy.

It was a few minutes before he moved or spoke. He lifted himself up on his elbows and pressed a soft kiss to her mouth. 'You are mine, Emma,' he said. 'Body and soul, you are mine.'

But for how long? Emma silently wondered as she kissed him back with all the tenderness she felt for him. She only hoped it would be long enough to melt the ice around his heart.

CHAPTER ELEVEN

OVER the next few weeks Emma found herself relaxing more and more into the role of Rafaele's wife. Lucia the housekeeper returned after her much-needed break, not even blinking an eye at Emma's occupation of Rafaele's suite of rooms. If anything she seemed rather pleased and smiled every time she encountered Emma.

'It is good,' Lucia said in her heavily accented voice. 'Signore Fiorenza would be very pleased. It is what he wanted for his son.'

Emma frowned as she helped the housekeeper fold some towels. 'What do you mean, Lucia?' she asked. 'Are you saying Signore Fiorenza Senior talked to you about the terms of his will?'

The housekeeper looked a little sheepish. 'He talk a little bit one night a week or two before he passed away,' she said. 'He wanted Rafaele to be happy. He think he wasting his life with loose women. He told me he thought you would make Rafaele a good wife. You are kind and gentle and would love him, not for his money, but for him.'

Emma stared at her. 'Signore Fiorenza told you that?'

'Yes, many times,' Lucia said. 'You are perfect for Rafaele, Signorina. You love him, *sì*? It has all worked out.'

Emma chewed at her lip with her teeth. 'Signore Fiorenza

was taking a big gamble,' she said. 'What if I hated his son on sight and refused to marry him?'

Lucia gave her a knowing look. 'Even if you had hated him you would not have watched his inheritance slip away,' she said. 'Signore Fiorenza knew that you would do the right thing by his son. He trusted you. And now it has worked out exactly as he planned. The Villa Fiorenza will soon be filled with yours and Rafaele's *bambinos*.'

Emma didn't have the heart to tell the housekeeper how unlikely that was. Instead she smiled and finished folding the towels, her heart aching for what could never be.

Over dinner a few evenings later Rafaele announced he had to travel back to London on business and would be away for a few days. Emma waited with bated breath for him to ask her to accompany him, but the request was not forthcoming. She sat as he talked about other things, her heart sinking so low she began to feel ill.

'You're not eating, *cara*,' he said, indicating her untouched meal. 'Do you not like Lucia's cooking?'

Emma gave him a forced smile and picked up her fork. 'Of course I do… It's lovely…'

'If you would prefer Carla to return that can be arranged,' he said. 'I am inclined to agree with you that this place is too much for Lucia.'

'I'm not sure Lucia would like to think she has reached her use by date,' Emma said. 'She loves it here. In any case I don't mind helping her with the heavier tasks.'

He frowned at her. '*Cara*, there is no need for you to scrub the floors and do the dishes. I pay other people to do those things. You are my wife.'

Emma gave him a weak smile. They had been married nearly seven weeks and she still didn't know if she would wake up tomorrow to find he had found someone else. It was like living with the sword of Damocles hanging over her head. She had even stopped saying she loved him. What was the point? He never said anything in return.

He reached for her hand and stroked his long fingers over the back of hers. 'You look pale, *tesore mio,*' he said. 'Have I been keeping you up too late at night, hmm?'

Emma suppressed a tiny shiver as his dark eyes speared hers meaningfully. The passion that flared so easily between them felt like another presence in the room; she could feel it circling the table, coming closer and closer until her body was quaking in reaction. Her legs felt shaky, her palms moist and her inner core melted as she thought of him pinning her with his hardness as he had done so earth-shatteringly earlier that evening. The experience of having him take her from behind had sent shock waves of delight rippling through her; the rough, almost primal coupling had sent shivers racing up and down her spine. He was a demanding and energetic lover, but a sensitive and considerate one. Just looking at him made her body tremble all over with desire, the skin on the back of her neck prickling as she thought of him driving into her warmth, taking her to the highest pinnacle of pleasure time and time again. Over the last few weeks together she had grown in sexual confidence, she knew how to pleasure him and delighted in doing so at every opportunity.

She didn't like thinking of him pleasuring other women in the past; instead she took what comfort she could in the fact he had been with her every night, his desire for her knowing no bounds.

Rafaele lifted her hand to his mouth, holding her gaze as he pressed her bent fingers to his lips. 'I would take you with me to London except I will be tied up in meetings the whole time,' he said. 'But I promise to take you somewhere else for a short break next month. Where would you like to go? Paris? Monaco perhaps?'

'Anywhere would be lovely,' Emma said softly. 'I just want to be with you.'

His fingers tightened momentarily on her hand. 'You are very sweet, Emma,' he said with a slight rasp in his voice. 'You deserve someone much nicer than me.'

'I don't want anyone else but you,' she insisted.

He released her hand and picked up his wineglass, his expression locking her out. 'I leave first thing in the morning,' he said. 'I will be back on Sunday or maybe even Monday, I am not sure.'

'You have meetings on a weekend?' Emma asked, not quite able to remove the air of suspicion in her tone.

His eyes became hard as they held hers. 'I hope this is not leading where I think it is leading.'

'Tell me something, Rafaele,' she said with an embittered look. 'Do you wake up each morning and tick another day off the calendar?'

'It's not like that at all,' he said with a frown.

She glared at him. 'Isn't it?'

'No, of course not,' he said. 'I enjoy having you around, Emma. You are good company.'

'Why don't you say what you really think?' she asked. 'It's not about the company and scintillating conversation I offer you, is it?'

His mouth was pulled tight. 'Don't do this, Emma.'

'It's the on-tap sex, isn't it, Rafaele?' she continued bitterly. 'Anywhere, any time, any position. That's what you want from me, isn't it? That's all you'll ever want from me, isn't it?'

'You are becoming hysterical,' he said with ice-cold calm.

'You called me a whore from the very first day,' she bit out resentfully, 'but what I didn't realise then was how quickly you would turn me into one.'

His brows snapped together. 'You are nothing of the sort,' he said. 'I have apologised for what I thought back then.'

'But you still think it, don't you?' she asked. 'Deep down inside there's still a part of you that won't accept I was just your father's carer. You see me as the conniving slut who stole half your inheritance, and nothing is going to change that, is it?'

'I do not think anything of the sort,' he clipped back. 'Emma, for God's sake, I am in absolutely no doubt I was your first lover. What sort of man do you think I am to doubt you after that?'

'You don't love me. You make love to me, but you don't love me.'

'I do not want to continue this discussion,' he said stiffly. 'You are not being reasonable.'

'I'll show you how reasonable I can be,' she said with another fiery glare as she pushed back from the table. 'I'm not going to wait around holding my breath for you to pull the rug from under my feet. I'm going to pack my bags and leave right now.'

The nerve flickered at his mouth again as he got to his feet. 'If you do I will make you regret it,' he said through clenched teeth. 'The press will hound you, I can guarantee it. What the Bennett family said about you in Australia will be nothing to what I will reveal about your activities here. I have contacts. One word from me and your reputation will be unsalvageable in any country.'

Emma stopped mid-stride, her stomach dropping in alarm. 'You would do it, wouldn't you?' she said. 'You heartless, selfish bastard, you would do it and think nothing of it, wouldn't you?'

His eyes glittered with steely purpose. 'If you walk out on me you will regret it, I guarantee it. Don't make me do it, Emma. I don't want to hurt you.'

She looked at him in disdain. 'Don't lie to me,' she bit out. 'You would take great pleasure in hurting me. I know you would.'

He put his hands on her shoulders and brought her towards him. 'Emma, listen to me,' he said, his tone now gentle. 'I do not want things to get ugly between us. We have been thrown together by the machinations of my father. That is not your fault and neither is it mine. It is fortunate we enjoy each other's company so that we can see this through in order to get what we both want.'

'But I can't have what I want, can I?' she asked with tears stinging her eyes. 'You don't love me…you're never going to love me…'

He let out a heavy sigh. 'I care for you, Emma,' he said. 'I know it is not quite the same as the three magic words you crave, but it is more than I have felt for any other woman I have been involved with before.'

'It's not enough,' Emma said. 'I thought it would be but it's not. I want to be loved. I want to feel secure. I can't live with this shadow of uncertainty hanging over me. I never know from one day to the next if it's going to be my last with you. You hold all the power in our relationship, which means you have the least to lose if the relationship fails.'

'I cannot give you what you want,' he said. 'I don't want the same things in life.'

'Only because you're afraid of being let down like you were before,' she said. 'You lost your mother when you were young. That is enough to shatter anyone's sense of security. Then you lost your brother in the most tragic of circumstances, leaving you with a father who was unable to function as a mature adult. Everyone you have ever loved has deserted you one way or the other. Can't you see how that has impacted on how you view all of your relationships?'

He dropped his hands from her shoulders as if she had burned him. 'I do not need you to psychoanalyse me, Emma,' he said tersely. 'I am well aware of my shortcomings. Now stop this nonsense and sit back down and eat your dinner.'

Emma resumed her seat and began to pick at her food, but her stomach churned as she forced each mouthful down. She wondered if this was what people described as lovesickness. The gnawing ache was almost unbearable; it made her feel clammy and faint. Eventually she gave up and, pushing the plate away, got to her feet. 'Will you excuse me?' she asked. 'I think I'll go to bed. I'm not feeling well.'

Rafaele rose from the table with a frown. 'You should have told me earlier,' he said. 'No wonder you have been so tetchy. What can I get you?'

'Nothing,' she said, putting a hand to her damp forehead. 'It's just a little headache. I'll be fine once I've had a rest.'

He came around and placed his arm around her waist, guiding her upstairs with the gentle solicitousness Emma found so very confusing since he maintained he didn't love her. 'I will sleep in one of the other rooms tonight so as not to disturb you,' he said.

'You don't have to do that,' she protested.

He gave her a wry smile. 'I have to leave at an ungodly hour in any case,' he said. 'Now get into bed and I will bring you a glass of water and some paracetamol.'

Emma crawled into the big bed and closed her eyes against the swirling nausea as she waited for him to return…

Rafaele came back into the bedroom to find Emma fast asleep, her face still far too pale, the bruise-like shadows beneath her closed eyes making his gut suddenly clench. He sat on the edge of the bed and, pushing the silky hair off her face, gently stroked her smooth brow. She made a child-like murmur and nestled against his hand, the movement so trusting he felt another blade of guilt slice through him. He should never have allowed things to go this far. She was young and inexperienced, of course she fancied herself in love with him. It wouldn't last, he was sure of it. And then where would he be? He wasn't used to feeling so vulnerable in a relationship. Every time he made love to her it was a totally new experience, his pleasure reaching heights it never had before. Seeing her blossom with sensuality was captivating, she was such a generous lover, shy but adventurous, her passion a perfect match for his.

But how could he give her what she wanted? She had no idea of how things had been set up. If she were to find out about the codicil to his father's will she would no longer be talking about loving him. She would hate him and how could he blame her?

He bent down and pressed a soft kiss to Emma's temple and she blinked sleepily and looked up at him. 'Rafaele?'

He brushed his thumb over her slightly parted lips. *'Qual e´ il mio piccolo?'* he asked.

She placed her hand over his and held it to her cheek. 'I'm going to miss you,' she said.

'Sto per perdere anche voi,' he said, and then translated, 'I am going to miss you too.'

The villa was achingly empty once Rafaele left the following morning. Emma heard him leave first thing and felt immediately disconsolate. The days stretched ahead of her interminably. She couldn't imagine how she would survive when their marriage was brought to its inevitable end.

She pulled back the covers and got to her feet but was so quickly assailed by a giant wave of nausea she stumbled to the *en suite* and was promptly sick. She staggered out after the bout of sickness was over, but she still felt so wretched she had to lie down again.

A little thought began to gnaw at her like a tiny mouse nibbling at a crumb, and, although she tried to ignore it, it wouldn't go away.

It couldn't be possible.

It *couldn't* be.

They had used protection.

She was back on the pill.

Her hand crept to her belly, her thoughts still whirling out of control. She couldn't remember the last time she had been physically sick. It didn't seem possible she could have fallen pregnant in such a short space of time.

Panic clutched at her insides with claw-like fingers. How could she tell Rafaele? He had never promised her anything but an affair. She had been the one to profess love, not him.

Emma knew she had to have a test before she worked herself into a state of hysteria. There was no point in worrying about something that might not have even happened. She could easily have picked up a bug of some sort. After all, she had worked tirelessly looking after Valentino Fiorenza; it had drained her more than she had realised, leaving her run-down and vulnerable.

She got dressed and walked down to the town centre to the nearest pharmacy and in her rather fractured Italian managed to relay to the assistant what she wanted. She felt every eye on her as she took her purchase and left, wondering if she had been wise to buy the test locally, given everyone knew she was Rafaele Fiorenza's new wife.

The test was positive.

Emma stared at it for several heart-chugging seconds, her pulse so heavy she felt every beat of it in her fingertips as they clutched at the basin in the *en suite*.

The phone started to ring in the bedroom and she left the test on the counter to answer it. *'Buongiorno, Villa Fiorenza.'*

'*Buongiorno*, Emma,' Rafaele said with a smile in his voice. 'I see you are practising your Italian.'

She ran her tongue over the dust-like dryness of her lips. 'How is your business trip?'

'It is the usual run of boring meetings,' he said. 'How are things with you?'

'Um…things are fine…' she said, trying to inject some life in her tone.

'You sound distracted, Emma.'

'I-I'm not.'

He gave a soft chuckle of laughter. 'Are you missing me, *tesore mio*?'

'Are you missing me?' Emma asked in return.

'What do you think?' he asked.

She felt the velvet drape of his voice all over her skin and suppressed a little shiver. 'I think you have probably found some way to distract yourself,' she said. 'I can't imagine you pining away in your hotel room all on your own.'

There was a small silence.

Emma heard the thud thud of her heartbeats and felt another wave of nausea wash over her. She swallowed thickly and clasped the phone a little tighter to keep control.

'You have no need to be jealous, Emma,' he said. 'I have told you before, I am not interested in anyone but you.'

'For the moment,' she said in an embittered tone.

He gave an impatient sigh. 'I have not got time for this. I have another meeting in a few minutes.'

'In the bedroom or the boardroom?' she asked.

This time the ensuing silence had a menacing quality to it.

'If you want me to find someone else to make the accusations you toss at me true, then that can easily be arranged,' he said. 'Is that what you want?'

What Emma really wanted was for him to love her the way

she loved him, but she knew it was pointless telling him. 'No…no, of course that's not what I want…' she said in a broken whisper.

'I want you, Emma,' he said in a tender tone. 'I wish you were here with me now.'

'I wish I was there too,' she said, caving into his charm. 'I miss you.' *And I am carrying your baby*, she wished she could add if circumstances were different.

'I will be back as soon as I can,' he said. 'Take care of yourself while I am away.'

'I will…'

There was another little pause.

'Emma?'

'Yes?'

'Nothing,' he said after a moment. 'It can wait. I will talk to you when I get back.'

Emma hung up the phone once he'd ended the call and went back to the *en suite*, and, picking up the pregnancy test, looked at it again to make sure she hadn't been imagining it. The truth stared back at her, making her heart pump with dread all over again…

CHAPTER TWELVE

EMMA was in the pool enjoying the peace of the evening when Rafaele returned. She hadn't heard his car on the gravel driveway and felt at a disadvantage when he came out to the deck and found her dripping wet as she hastily tried to wrap a towel around herself.

His hands stilled her clumsy movements and the towel slipped to deck at her feet. 'You don't have to be shy with me, Emma,' he said. 'I like seeing your body. It is beautiful.'

Emma felt suddenly exposed. Could he see how her breasts were slightly bigger? she wondered. Her cheeks grew hot under his lazy scrutiny and one of her hands crept to the flat plane of her belly, just to reassure herself there was no sign of the tiny life growing there.

He bent his head and kissed her soundly on the mouth. 'You know something, Emma?' he said, looking down at her with that sooty gaze of his. 'Right now all I want to do is kiss you and take you to bed. I have missed you more than I realised.'

Emma could feel herself weakening and nestled closer, her arms going about his neck to bring his mouth down to her. 'I missed you too…so much.'

His mouth connected with hers in a prolonged kiss of passion, his tongue thrusting against hers in a sexy motion that sent her senses spinning out of control. His hands cupped her breasts, moulding and shaping them possessively until she was boneless in his arms. She felt his erection pressing against her, its rock-hard presence a heady reminder of all the pleasure he had shown her before.

He lifted his mouth off hers to kiss her neck before going lower to where her breasts ached for his attention. He undid her bikini top and suckled on her tantalisingly, her nipples pushing against his tongue in their eagerness. She whimpered as he turned his attention to her other breast, his hot mouth like a brand on her quivering flesh.

He placed his hands on her hips, bringing her against him as his mouth returned to hers with renewed vigour.

Emma rubbed up against him feverishly, her body clamouring for his possession. Every nerve ending was screaming out for release, her body so ready for him she felt the humidity of her need between her thighs.

As if he sensed her growing urgency he helped her out of her bikini bottoms, his fingers searching for her slick warmth with devastating accuracy. She squirmed as he touched the tight pearl of need, the sensations rocketing through her.

Just when she thought she could stand it no more he suddenly turned her around. Emma's breath locked in her throat as she heard his zipper come down. She whimpered in excitement as he parted her legs for his entry, the anticipation of that first deep thrust almost sending her over the edge then and there.

He surged forward, a deep groan of pleasure bursting from his mouth as her tight muscles clenched around him. 'God, I have been dreaming of this the whole time I was away,' he said, grasping her by the waist to keep her in place.

Emma was beyond speech. Each rocking thrust was bringing her closer to the ecstasy she longed for, his guttural, almost primal sounds of pleasure like music to her ears. She felt him search for her again, those long, clever fingers intensifying the sensations until she was panting breathlessly as the first waves of release began to wash over her. She shuddered convulsively, the hard, repeated thrusts pitching her headlong into an orgasm so intense it was like fireworks going off in her head.

He kept pumping; his strong thighs braced either side of hers, his fingers digging into her waist as the pressure inexorably built. Emma shivered as she felt him get closer; she loved that moment when he finally lost control. It was the only time he ever allowed himself to be vulnerable; it made her feel as if she was the only woman in the world who could do that to him.

With one last groan he was there, the breath going out of him as his essence spilled into her tight warmth, his chest rising and falling against her back as he held her in the aftermath.

Emma breathed in the musky scent of him, the sensation of his fluid between her thighs intensely erotic.

His hands moved from her waist to cup her breasts, his body still joined to hers. 'I should have used a condom,' he said, 'but I couldn't wait. That is how much you affect me.'

Emma could feel herself tensing and forced herself to relax. 'I'm sure it will be OK…'

He began to nuzzle beneath her left ear. 'You smell so nice,' he said. 'Like orange blossom with just a hint of chlorine.'

She gave a little shiver as his tongue circled the shell of her ear. 'Maybe we should go upstairs,' she said somewhat breathlessly. 'I wouldn't want Lucia to see us like this.'

'She has gone home for the day,' Rafaele said as he pressed his mouth to the nape of her neck. 'She was leaving as I came in.'

Emma tilted her head sideways, her skin breaking out in

goose-bumps as his lips and tongue moved over her. She felt his body thickening again and her belly began to quiver in reaction.

'Can you feel what you are doing to me, Emma?' he asked against her neck.

She began to writhe as he moved against her. 'Yes…'

'I can never seem to get enough of you,' he said, rocking back and forth, slowly at first, his body growing harder with each movement.

Emma started to gasp as his speed picked up. Her legs were trembling as his hands went to her hips, her inner core so alive with nerve endings every surging movement of his body within hers made her quake in delight.

'Do you like it like this, Emma?' he asked as his thumbs rolled over her tight nipples.

'Yes,' she said, sucking in a breath as he thrust deeper. 'Oh, yes…'

'You like how I make you feel, don't you, *cara*?' he asked.

Emma whimpered again as he drove harder. 'You know I do…'

His hands went back to her hips, his fingers splayed possessively. 'Your body fits mine perfectly,' he said. 'I like the feel of you skin on skin. Yours reminds me of silk, so soft and smooth under my fingertips.'

Emma shuddered as his fingers found her feminine cleft, the coaxing motion against her sensitised flesh making her breathless with excitement. She couldn't hold back her response, it hit her in a series of pounding waves, tossing her about like a bit of flotsam, her body so spent she felt limbless.

She felt him shudder his way through his release, the sheer force of it reverberating through her body where it was pressed against his.

After a long quiet moment he moved back and gently turned her in his arms. 'Why don't you go upstairs and have a shower while I make a couple of calls?' he said. 'I will not be long.'

Emma felt her doubts returning and wondered who he intended calling at this time of night. 'I can wait with you while you make the calls,' she offered.

His expression became mask-like, but not before she saw that camera shutter flicker in his eyes. 'No, Emma,' he said, re-zipping his trousers. 'I have some private matters to discuss with a client. It would not be appropriate for me to conduct such a conversation within the hearing of someone else.'

'This is how it's always going to be, isn't it, Rafaele?' she asked bitterly. 'You're content to make love to me, but not to share any other aspect of your life.'

His mouth tightened. 'Watch it, Emma,' he said. 'You are starting to bore me with this jealous wife routine.'

'Why don't you send me away, then, Rafaele?' she said. 'Why not dismiss me from your life like all your other mistresses?'

He stood looking down at her with a nerve ticking at the corner of his mouth. 'I do not need this right now. I have only just walked in the door; I do not want to be drawn into a pointless argument with you.'

She gave him a churlish look. 'You won't give me anything but your body. It's not enough, Rafaele. I want more.'

He let out an impatient sound. 'I am going to the study,' he said. 'I will see you in the morning.'

'So you've finished with me for this evening, have you?' she sniped at him. 'You've slaked your lust and now I'm to go away like a good little whore until you need me to service you again.'

A hard look came into his eyes. 'I have not treated you as a whore and you damn well know it.'

She turned away in distress. 'Sometimes I wish I still hated you. It would be so much easier than this…'

Emma felt him come up behind her, his hands coming to rest on her shoulders. 'I do not want you to hate me, Emma,' he said gently. 'That is not what I want at all.'

She turned back to face him. 'But you don't want me to love you either, do you?'

The pads of his thumbs moved in a slow caress of her cheeks as he cupped her face in his hands. 'Love is something I am not so sure of,' he said. 'People say they love each other all the time and the next day they are at each other's throats. How can anyone know if what they feel is genuine?'

Emma looked into his dark eyes. 'I can't speak for other people, but I know what I mean when I say I love you.'

His eyes searched hers for a long moment before he released her. 'Go to bed, *cara*,' he said softly. 'I will be up shortly.'

Emma turned over in bed early the following morning to find Rafaele propped up on one elbow looking at her. She shoved her tussled hair out of her eyes and gave him a coy smile as she thought of the tumultuous passion they had shared the night before when he had finally come up to bed. She trailed her fingers from his sternum towards his groin as she had done only hours ago.

He captured her hand and held it against his chest. 'There is something we need to discuss,' he said in a tone deep with gravitas.

Emma felt her stomach lurch. She looked at him uncertainly, her heart thumping so hard she was sure he would feel the blood pounding in her fingertips where they were pressed against him. 'Y-yes?' she said in a scratchy whisper.

His dark, inscrutable eyes were steady on hers. 'Why didn't you tell me you are not on the pill?' he asked.

Emma stared at him in silence for several heart-chugging seconds, her mouth growing dry.

'Why, Emma?' he asked, his expression darkening with what looked suspiciously like anger. 'You have had numerous opportunities to tell me, but you have not done so.'

Emma swallowed unevenly. 'I…how do you know I'm not on it?'

This time the anger was unmistakable. She could see a jackhammer-like pulse beating at the corner of his white-tipped mouth. 'Because I looked, that is why,' he said.

She rolled her lips together for a moment. 'Looked where?' she asked.

'In your toiletries bag in the bathroom,' he answered. 'There was no sign of any contraceptives in that or your handbag and I would like to know why.'

Emma pulled out of his hold and got off the bed to glare down at him. 'I would like to know why you think you have the right to search through my belongings without my permission.'

His mouth tightened even further as he stood up and faced her squarely. 'You gave me the right when you agreed to be my lover,' he said. 'Now answer me, damn you. Why didn't you tell me?'

'It's none of your business, that's why,' Emma said, stung at the brutish manner of his inquisition. This wasn't going anything like she had planned, she thought in despair. She had wanted to prepare him, to wait until she felt secure enough to deliver her bombshell, but somehow he had pre-empted her.

His eyes narrowed into dark slits. 'You are trying to trap me, aren't you, Emma?'

Emma felt frighteningly close to tears. 'No, that's not true. We've always used condoms and I know this isn't for ever so I just thought—'

'You just thought what?' he barked at her savagely.

She flinched and shrank back against the wall. 'I-I thought it would be all right…'

'When was your last period?'

She turned away, nausea rising like a tide inside her.

He let out a vicious expletive and strode around the bed to grasp her by the upper arms, his fingers biting into her flesh almost cruelly. 'Think, damn it! When was it?'

Tears stung at the backs of her eyes. 'Stop,' she choked. 'You're hurting me.'

His grip loosened a fraction, but his expression was still livid. 'You have done this deliberately, haven't you? For all I know you could already be pregnant.'

Emma swallowed convulsively and averted her gaze from the searing blaze of his, her heart hammering, her skin beading with nervous perspiration.

The silence was suddenly so intense it rang like clanging bells inside her head.

Rafaele bit out a rough expletive and brought her face back in line with his gaze. 'You are, aren't you?' he said, and after a tight pause added hoarsely, '*Mio Dio*…you already are.'

She ran her tongue over her lips. 'I don't know how it happened,' she said. 'We used a condom every single time…you know we did, apart from yesterday by the pool.'

'And apart from the first time,' he reminded her coolly.

She looked at him in confusion. 'But you didn't…you know…come inside me that time.'

'There are literally thousands of sperm in pre-ejaculatory fluid,' he said. 'It only takes one to do the job.'

Emma bit her lip until she tasted blood. 'I'm sorry…'

He stepped away from her. 'I should have known you would try something like this,' he ground out. 'How long have you known?'

She swallowed again. 'I did a test a couple of days ago…'

His eyes glittered with fury. 'And you didn't think to tell me?'

'I-I was going to but…but I was frightened you would be angry.'

'Have I not the right to be angry?' he asked as he reached for his clothes.

Emma watched as he dressed, her heart feeling like a cold, hard stone in her chest. 'I'm not getting rid of it,' she suddenly blurted into the stiff silence. 'You can't make me.'

He left his shirt hanging undone as he came over to where she was still standing. 'Do you really think I would demand that of you?' he asked, frowning heavily.

She gave him a pointed look. 'Wouldn't you?'

He blew out a breath and sent his hand through his hair once more. 'I might be a bit of a bastard at times, but surely you don't think I am that big a one.'

'I don't know what to think…' she said. 'I didn't expect this to happen.'

'No?' he asked with a cynical curl of his lip. 'A temporary marriage was not enough for you was it, Emma? You wanted a child thrown in to make things really interesting.'

'How can you think that of me?' she asked in rising despair. 'From day one you set about to seduce me. You assumed I was a slut and made it your business to get me into bed to prove your point. The way I see it my being pregnant is your fault rather than mine.'

His jaw clenched so hard Emma heard his teeth grind together. 'So you wanted to make me pay and pay dearly for misjudging you,' he said through tight lips. 'What better way than to make sure I was tied to you permanently.'

'I wouldn't want my baby to be exposed to someone so incapable of loving it,' she threw back.

His mouth was a thin, flat line of anger. 'You seem to be forgetting something, Emma,' he said in a chilling tone. 'If you are in fact expecting a child it will be mine just as much as yours. I will have just as much say as you in its upbringing, perhaps, given my financial position and legal contacts, even more so.'

Emma felt a quake of alarm rumble through her. She knew he was more than capable of doing what he threatened. The courts were much more accommodating of fathers' rights these days. He wouldn't have much difficulty convincing the authorities he would be a more suitable custodian, especially since the press hadn't done her any favours in how they had reported the Bennett family's aspersions on her character. She would have a mammoth fight on her hands if she took him on in a legal battle, and she already knew who would be the loser…

'This is not the way my life is supposed to be,' she said, trying not to cry. 'The only man I've ever slept with is you and now…' her chin gave a little wobble and her eyes sprouted tears '…and now I wish to God I hadn't.'

He placed his hands on her shoulders before she could spin away. 'I am sorry, Emma,' he said in a gruff tone. 'I am being an unfeeling bastard as usual.'

Emma gave a little sniff and burrowed closer, her cheek pressed flat against the thudding of his heart, her arms going around his bare waist beneath his open shirt. She felt his breath disturb the top of her head and felt his chest rise and fall in a sigh. One of his hands began stroking the back of her head, the movement so tender she wondered all over again if somewhere deep inside, in spite of all his denials, he felt a smidgeon of affection for her.

'I am not doing a great job of this, am I?' he asked in self-deprecation. 'All I seem to do is make you cry.'

She lifted her face off his chest to look up at him. 'It's all right,' she said. 'I know this is difficult for you.'

Rafaele brushed her hair back off her forehead. It was going to be much more difficult for her, he reflected, frowning as he thought of the implications for her. She was thousands of kilometres away from her only family, her sister and her niece; married to a man she had met a little less than two months ago, a man who had treated her like trash and yet she claimed to love him.

Did he deserve such a woman?

Would the curse he had had on others' lives impact on hers? Hadn't it already?

'This changes everything,' he said, surprised his voice came out at all, let alone sounding so in command. The truth was he wasn't in command. He had tried to keep his life simple, no ties, no false promises, no guarantees…no love…

Rafaele realised with a lightning-like jolt that he wanted to be loved, but, more than that, he wanted it to last. He had spent so many years avoiding being disappointed, long, lonely years locking his heart away in case someone let him down while he wasn't on guard. Emma had somehow pierced that firewall and caused utter mayhem with his rigidly controlled emotions. She had turned his neatly ordered world upside down. He would never be the same again now she had come into his life. If she walked away now it would destroy him. His gut clenched at the thought of revealing his vulnerability to her. Would she use it to exploit him? How could he be sure?

'What do you mean this changes everything?' she asked, looking at him with a worried pleat of her brow.

'Our marriage will not be temporary,' he told her.

Emma's eyes went wide. 'N-not temporary?'

'We have a child on the way,' he said. 'We will continue our relationship in order to raise him or her the way neither of us was raised—with love and solid commitment from both its parents. It is important that our marriage from hence forth be as normal as possible.'

'This is hardly what anyone would call a normal marriage.' Emma felt the need to remind him.

He pulled her closer towards him. 'I do not know about that,' he said, resting one hand on the small of her back. 'It feels rather normal to me. You are wearing my ring, you have taken my name and you have my child in your womb.'

'But you don't love me.' She addressed the words to his chest, her heart contracting with pain.

He tipped up her face, his eyes holding hers. 'That is everything to you, isn't it? You want the words, but aren't the actions far more important?'

Emma felt her breath come to a halt in her chest. 'W-what are you saying?'

His mouth twisted ruefully as he brushed another tendril of hair off her face. 'To tell you the truth, I am not sure,' he said. 'All I know is I have never felt like this before with any other woman.'

Emma blinked back tears. She knew a pregnancy wasn't an ideal reason for staying in a loveless marriage; children put a strain on even the strongest relationships, but she knew Rafaele would not do anything to compromise his child's welfare, certainly not after what he had experienced in his own childhood. She had every confidence he would fall in love with his son or daughter on sight, hoping against hope that perhaps in time he might come to feel something deeper for her than sexual desire.

'I will try to be a good wife for you,' she said. 'I know this isn't what you wanted, but I will do my best to support you and our child.'

'Do you think it will be a boy or a girl?' he asked.

'I don't know and it's too early to tell, but would you like to know before the birth?'

'What would you prefer?'

'I think I'd like to be surprised,' she said. 'But if you want to know beforehand I won't stop you.'

He gathered her close. 'I have to go to Milan today to sort out some legal business.'

Emma looked at him hopefully. 'Can I come with you?'

He held her gaze for an infinitesimal moment. 'Not this time, *mio piccolo*. I have to leave now.'

'But I would like to come with you,' she said. 'I could do some shopping or something while you see to your business.'

'No, Emma.' This time his tone was implacable. 'I want you to take care of yourself. You are carrying my child, don't forget. I would not like anything to compromise his or her well-being. That is after all why we are staying together, is it not?'

Emma felt his words like a stinging slap across the face. 'Oh, yes,' she said with a querulous look. 'How could I forget?'

He reached for his bathrobe and tied the ends together. 'I am not going to be goaded into a fight. I realise this is a rocky time for you during early pregnancy. Your hormones and your emotions are all over the place.'

'My emotions are all over the place because I don't know where I stand with you,' she threw back tearfully.

He drew in an impatient breath. 'All right,' he said, raking his hand through his hair. 'I love you. Does that make you feel better?'

'You d-don't mean it,' Emma said and started to cry. 'Y-you're only saying it to placate me.'

He muttered a curse and came over to her, hauling her into his arms and holding her close. 'I mean it, Emma,' he said gruffly. 'I love you. I am not used to revealing my feelings. I have never allowed it to happen before. But I do love you.'

Emma desperately wanted to believe him, but how could

she be sure? He now had what he had wanted: the villa was in his hands. Even if they divorced he would still maintain possession of the bulk of his father's estate.

He dropped a kiss on the top of her head. 'Go back to bed, *cara*,' he said gently. 'I will bring you some tea and toast before I leave.'

Emma crawled back into bed, annoyed with herself for pushing him. She had been so desperate for a confession of love, but now she had it she felt let down and empty. Was it always going to be this way between them, her pushing and him pulling away?

CHAPTER THIRTEEN

WHEN Emma woke a couple of hours later Rafaele had left, but she was touched to see a plate of toast and a cup of tea sitting on the bedside table next to her. Even though it was lukewarm she sipped at the tea and nibbled on the toast until her stomach began to settle.

After her shower she went down to the town centre to make an appointment at the medical clinic for a pregnancy check-up. The female doctor was heavily booked but the receptionist was able to squeeze Emma in for the following day.

Emma was coming out of the clinic with her appointment card in her hand when she saw a woman coming towards her rather purposefully.

'Signora Fiorenza,' the woman said, coming to stand in front of Emma, more or less blocking her escape. 'Do you have a moment?'

'Y-yes?' Emma said, hoping the woman wasn't a journalist. 'How can I help you?'

'We have not met, but I am sure you have heard of me,' the woman said. 'My name is Sondra Henning.'

Emma felt a flicker of alarm like an electric current run up her spine. She didn't like the ice-cold blue of the woman's eyes, nor did she care for the thin-lipped smile.

'Yes…I have heard of you,' she said and offered her hand. 'How do you do?'

Sondra's hand was like a cold fish against hers. 'It's all worked out rather nicely for Rafaele, hasn't it?' she said. 'He couldn't have asked for a more biddable wife.'

Emma frowned. 'I'm not sure what you mean…'

Sondra's smile didn't reach her eyes. 'You agreed to the terms of his father's will, in good faith, I imagine, but then perhaps he hasn't told you about the codicil to Valentino's will.'

Emma felt her stomach tilt sideways. 'W-what codicil?'

Sondra's cat-like gaze ran over Emma insolently. 'Valentino knew Rafaele was a playboy with no intention of ever settling down so at the last minute he added a codicil to his will. It stated that on the event of his marriage to you he would become the principal shareholder of Valentino's investment company. It is worth several million, a nice little inducement to matrimony, don't you think?'

Emma swallowed against a thick tide of rising nausea. 'I don't believe you,' she said. 'I was never informed of any codicil by the lawyer who handled the will.'

Sondra's lip curled. 'That is because Valentino insisted you were not to see it,' she said. 'He wanted nature to take its course, so to speak. He knew you would fall in love with Rafaele, most women do, but what he was not so sure of was whether Rafaele would fall in love with you.'

'He has fallen in love with me,' Emma said. 'He told me so this morning.'

Sondra gave her a pitying look. 'Oh, dear,' she drawled. 'You have got it bad, haven't you, my dear? Of course he would say he loved you. And perhaps he does in a way. After all, you have made him a very rich man.'

'He doesn't need any more wealth,' Emma said in a desperate attempt to defend Rafaele. 'I don't believe he would have acted so callously. I don't believe it.'

'You can always call the lawyer and find out for yourself,' Sondra said. 'Now that you have been married to Rafaele for a couple of months there would be no reason to keep it under wraps.'

'How do you know so much about all this?' Emma asked. 'You haven't been intimately involved with Valentino Fiorenza for years and as far as I recall you never once visited him while I was taking care of him.'

'Ah, but I did visit him and regularly,' Sondra said with a smugness Emma found offensive. 'And as to being involved with him…' She gave another conceited look. 'There are different levels of involvement. It was in my interests to keep Valentino as a trusted friend and confidante. After all, we had a history, one I wasn't keen on him disregarding when it came to the issue of his will.'

Emma felt the cold hand of contempt clutch at her insides at the avaricious tone of the other woman's voice. 'But I don't recall you ever coming to the palazzo in Milan, and Lucia has never once mentioned you coming to see him at the villa here.'

Sondra gave Emma a cold-hearted sneer. 'That old crone is too old to be looking after a place the size of The Villa Fiorenza,' she said. 'She doesn't see the dust on the chandeliers let alone who walks in and out of the back entrance. And as for the palazzo in Milan, that was all too easy. I phoned Valentino whenever you were out on an errand. I had an agreement with Rosa the housemaid there.'

Emma's insides tightened even further. 'An…an agreement?'

Sondra's smile was all the more sneering. 'Rosa always let

me know when you were going out so I could talk to Valentino in privacy on the telephone.'

Emma was still frowning so hard she felt an ache between her eyes. 'If you were so close to Valentino why didn't he ever mention to me you had phoned or visited him?'

'I asked him not to, that's why. I told him I was dating a very jealous man who wouldn't understand my continued affection for an ex-lover. Fortunately for me, Valentino agreed to our little secret. I think it fed his ego that I had never stopped caring about him. In any case, he knew what the paparazzi were like given what they had reported about his supposed involvement with you. As I was one of the few friends he had he didn't want to cause trouble for me.'

'Is that why you didn't come to his funeral?' Emma asked. 'Because of what your new lover might think?'

Sondra inspected her talon-like nails, her gaze averted, Emma suspected deliberately. 'I wanted to remember Valentino as he was the last time I saw him,' Sondra said, but her tone lacked sincerity.

'When *was* the last time you saw him?' Emma asked.

Sondra returned her cold gaze to Emma's. 'It was a couple of weeks before he died,' she said. 'I had to wait until you left the villa to get more medication or whatever errand you were running. Lucia was out talking to one of the gardeners so I let myself in. It was then Valentino told me what he had decided to do.'

Emma frowned again. 'You mean about the will?'

'No,' Sondra said with a glint in her cold eyes, 'about his relationship with Rafaele.'

Something about the woman's cat-with-the-canary smile bothered Emma. 'What do you mean?'

'Valentino told me he had just written a long letter to his son,' Sondra said. 'In it he had begged for Rafaele's forgiveness for how he had treated him over his mother's and then his brother's death. It seems you had worked some sort of miracle on Valentino's hardened soul, Emma. He said as much himself. He decided he wanted to put things right before he died. He knew he didn't have long to go.'

'I don't remember him asking me to post a letter to his son,' Emma said. 'And I'm sure if he had got Lucia to do it she would have told me about it.'

'That is because he didn't ask you or Lucia to post it,' Sondra said with a malicious glint in her eyes.

Emma felt her heart begin to slam against her sternum. 'Who...who did he ask to post it?' she said, her voice coming out slightly strangled.

'Oh, Emma.' Sondra gave a cackling laugh. 'Valentino was right. You *are* as innocent as a dove.'

Emma's skin began to prickle all over. 'You took the letter...' she said hollowly. 'You took the letter but...but you didn't post it...'

Sondra's expression turned bitter. 'Of course I didn't post it. Valentino Fiorenza broke my heart. He refused to marry me. He wanted a mistress, not a wife. No one was ever going to replace his beloved Gabriela. Do you know what that was like for me? I was competing with a dead woman and there was no way I could win.'

'So you waited all this time to get back at him in the most despicable way,' Emma said, her stomach churning with disgust. 'You pretended to still care about him in those last months of his life just so you could have your revenge.'

'Revenge, as they say, is a dish best served cold,' Sondra said with a disaffected smile. 'And you can't get any colder than a dead man in his grave, now, can you?'

Emma swallowed back a mouthful of bile. 'When did you find out about the codicil?'

'That was only recently,' Sondra said. 'I have a friend who works in the legal firm handling Valentino's affairs.'

'That's a breach of client confidence,' Emma pointed out. 'Your friend could be criminally charged.'

Sondra gave another careless shrug. 'That is of no concern to me.'

Emma set her mouth. 'What exactly is your concern?' she asked.

'I am offering you a chance to get back at Rafaele for using you,' she said. 'If you leave him before the year is up I will let you retain your half share of the villa. And if you choose to sell it I will pay you double what he offers for it. I have some money an uncle left me. We could both have our revenge on the Fiorenza men—what do you say?'

'I say no,' Emma said coldly. 'I will have no part in hurting Rafaele even more than he has already been hurt. What you did is unforgivable, not just to Rafaele, but to Valentino. He waited in vain for his son to contact him. It broke his heart, I am sure of it. He went to his grave believing his son hadn't forgiven him. That is no doubt why he never talked about it with me. He felt such a failure as a father. He was so bitterly disappointed. So terribly hurt. How could you do that? How can you live with yourself?'

Sondra opened her handbag and pulled out an envelope with a broken Fiorenza wax seal on the back. 'Give that to that arrogant bastard of a husband of yours,' she said. 'Better late than never, right?'

Emma clutched the envelope with a shaky hand, her heart feeling so heavy she could scarcely breathe, watching in silence as Sondra Henning strode off just as purposefully as she had approached, until she rounded a corner and disappeared.

* * *

Emma was waiting for Rafaele in the salon when he returned from Milan. He came in carrying a bunch of blood-red roses and handed them to her with a wry smile. 'For you, *mio piccolo*,' he said. 'For being so patient with me.'

Emma took the roses and put them to one side. 'Rafaele...I need to talk to you,' she said, 'about the codicil on your father's will.'

Had his expression become shuttered or was she imagining it? Emma wondered as she searched his face.

'How did you find out about that?' he asked after a small but tense pause.

'I ran into Sondra Henning this morning in town,' she told him. 'She came over and introduced herself. She said you had agreed to marry me, not just because of the villa, but because you stood to gain millions from your father's company. Is that true?'

Rafaele let out his breath in a long uneven stream. 'I knew once you found out about that wretched codicil you would think that,' he said. 'That is why I went to Milan this morning. I met with the lawyers and set up a trust in your name. You are now the principal shareholder of my father's company until such time as our child is able to take control.'

Emma's mouth dropped open. 'I don't believe it...'

He gave her a crooked smile. 'Why is it you do not believe a word I say, *mio piccolo*?' he asked. 'I finally summon up the courage to tell you I love you and you think I am fibbing. How on earth am I going to convince you it is true?'

She blinked back tears of happiness. 'You really mean it, don't you?' she asked. 'You really love me.'

He blocked the pathway of her tears with the pad of his thumb. 'I love you so much it hurts,' he said in a husky tone. 'I did not think I had the capacity to love so deeply. For years

I had shut myself off from feeling. But you, *cara*, with your big heart and caring ways, changed all that.'

'Oh, Rafaele…' Emma said. 'There's something else Sondra Henning told me…'

He went very still as if he sensed what was coming. Emma took a breath and in a gentle voice told him about the letter his father had written to him and how the wicked spitefulness of Sondra Henning had ruined any chance of Valentino making peace with his son. When she had finished, Emma handed him the letter with tears in her eyes.

'Have you read it?' Rafaele asked.

She shook her head. 'No, that letter was meant for you, no one else.'

He gave her a smile that was shaded by sadness. 'Would you excuse me for a moment or two?' he asked.

'Of course,' she said softly. 'Please…take your time.'

He went over by the bank of windows and opened the unsealed envelope, his eyes travelling down each page until he came to the end.

It seemed a long time before he looked back at Emma and when he did she could see the film of moisture in his eyes, making her own tears run all the more profusely.

Rafaele came back to stand in front of her. 'I do not know how to thank you, Emma, for what you have done,' he said.

She creased her brow at him. 'What have *I* done?'

He touched her face with his fingertips. 'You are an angel, do you know that? An angel sent down to this planet to make stubborn people like my father and I change our ways. If it had not been for you I would still hate my father. I would still be blaming him for all that was wrong in my life.'

Her eyes were glistening with tears. 'You don't hate him any more?'

He shook his head. 'Even if I had not seen this letter I had already decided to forgive him,' he said. 'You were so right when you said he was consumed by grief. He loved my mother so much he couldn't cope with the shock of her loss. There was no grief counselling in those days, he soldiered on in the only way he knew how, which was to bury himself in bitterness and denial.

'And then he was hit with the blow of Giovanni's accidental death. He blamed himself; he says so in the letter. He felt guilty that he hadn't been an involved father, leaving us for long periods on our own while he worked too hard and too long. His affair with Sondra Henning was his attempt to find a replacement mother for me after Giovanni's death, but of course it backfired. She wasn't interested in mothering some other woman's child. She wanted him to herself, but he would never agree to it. That proves more than anything how much he cared for me.'

'Oh, darling,' Emma said, tearing up again. 'You have been through so much.'

'He loved me, Emma,' Rafaele said, still trying to get his head around the fact. 'He loved me but just didn't know how to communicate it.'

Emma lifted her hand to his face and gently stroked the stubbly growth on his cheek. 'Now who does that remind you of?'

He smiled and pulled her close. 'Now, about that honeymoon we never had. Where would you like to go? I have cleared my diary so I am all yours for as long as you want.'

Emma looked up at him with love shining in her eyes. 'How long does a normal honeymoon last?' she asked with a playful smile.

He gave her a sexy grin in return. 'I do not really know,

but I can tell you one thing for sure,' he said, and paused as he planted a kiss on the end of her nose.

'What's that?' she asked, wrinkling her nose in delight.

He scooped her up in his arms and carried her towards the stairs, his dark eyes smouldering with passion. 'This one is going to last for ever.'

MILLS & BOON
MODERN™

On sale 2nd January 2009

INNOCENT MISTRESS, ROYAL WIFE
by Robyn Donald

Prince Rafiq de Couteveille of Moraze blames Alexa Considine
for his sister's death and is out for revenge. Lexie can't
understand why she's attracted the Prince's attention.
However, Rafiq is irresistible, and she soon finds
herself bedded by royalty…

TAKEN FOR REVENGE, BEDDED FOR PLEASURE
by India Grey

Gorgeous Olivier Moreau has only one reason for
seducing innocent Bella Lawrence. However, when cold
revenge becomes red-hot passion, Olivier finds he
has no intention of letting her go…

THE BILLIONAIRE BOSS'S INNOCENT BRIDE
by Lindsay Armstrong

Max Goodwin needs a glamorous secretary – fast – and when
dowdy employee Alexandra Hill transforms into Cinderella, Max's
thoughts turn decidedly personal! However, Alex refuses to be
a mistress to anyone and Max will never take a wife…

THE BILLIONAIRE'S DEFIANT WIFE
by Amanda Browning

Prim and proper Aimi Carteret has put her tragic past
behind her. Now wealthy businessman Jonah Berkeley will
stop at nothing to breach her defences and get the feisty
woman he knows is underneath out and into his bed!

Celebrate 100 years of pure reading pleasure with Mills & Boon®

To mark our centenary, each month we're publishing a special 100th Birthday Edition. These celebratory editions are packed with extra features and include a FREE bonus story.

Plus, you have the chance to enter a fabulous monthly prize draw. See 100th Birthday Edition books for details.

Now that's worth celebrating!

September 2008
Crazy about her Spanish Boss by Rebecca Winters
Includes FREE bonus story
Rafael's Convenient Proposal

November 2008
**The Rancher's Christmas Baby
by Cathy Gillen Thacker**
Includes FREE bonus story *Baby's First Christmas*

December 2008
One Magical Christmas by Carol Marinelli
Includes FREE bonus story *Emergency at Bayside*

Look for Mills & Boon® 100th Birthday Editions at your favourite bookseller or visit
www.millsandboon.co.uk

FREE!

4 Books
and a surprise gift!

We would like to take this opportunity to thank you for reading this Mills & Boon® book by offering you the chance to take FOUR more specially selected titles from the Modern™ series absolutely FREE! We're also making this offer to introduce you to the benefits of the Mills & Boon® Book Club™ —

★ **FREE home delivery**
★ **FREE gifts and competitions**
★ **FREE monthly Newsletter**
★ **Exclusive Mills & Boon Book Club offers**
★ **Books available before they're in the shops**

Accepting these FREE books and gift places you under no obligation to buy, you may cancel at any time, even after receiving your free shipment. Simply complete your details below and return the entire page to the address below. You don't even need a stamp!

YES! Please send me 4 free Modern books and a surprise gift. I understand that unless you hear from me, I will receive 6 superb new titles every month for just £2.99 each, postage and packing free. I am under no obligation to purchase any books and may cancel my subscription at any time. The free books and gift will be mine to keep in any case.

P8ZEF

Ms/Mrs/Miss/Mr ....Initials ....

Surname ....

Address ....

BLOCK CAPITALS PLEASE

....

....Postcode ....

Send this whole page to:
UK: FREEPOST CN81, Croydon, CR9 3WZ